If the Haunting Fits, Wear It

Rose Pressey

KENSINGTON PUBLISHING CORP.

http://www.kensingtonbooks.com

KENSINGTON BOOKS are published by

Kensington Publishing Corp.
119 West 40th Street
New York, NY 10018

All Kensington titles, imprints and distributed lines are available at special quantity discounts for bulk purchases for sales promotions, premiums, fund-raising, and educational or institutional use. Special book excerpts or customized printings can also be created to fit specific needs. For details, write or phone the office of the Kensington Special Sales Manager. Kensington Publishing Corp., 119 West 40th Street, New York, NY 10018. Attn.: Special Sales Department. Phone: 1-800-221-2647.

Kensington and the K logo Reg. U.S. Pat & TM Off.

ISBN-13: 978-1-4967-0555-6
ISBN-10: 1-4967-0555-6
First Kensington Mass Market Edition: July 2017

eISBN-13: 978-1-4967-0556-3
eISBN-10: 1-4967-0556-4
First Kensington Electronic Edition: July 2017

10 9 8 7 6 5 4 3 2 1

Printed in the United States of America

Also by Rose Pressey

The Haunted Vintage Mystery Series

To my son,
the kindest, most wonderful person
I've ever known.
He motivates me every day.
He's the love of my life.

Chapter 1

Grandma Pearl's Pearls of Wisdom

You gotta risk it to get the biscuit.

"Come one step closer and I'll kill you," I said.

The giant black, hairy spider didn't listen as he scurried toward me. I ran in the opposite direction. The creature was the size of a rat and probably would have survived any attempts I made to extinguish it. The best option for me was to let him run off into the little dark corner he came from. I'd grab what I came into the attic for, and we'd both be happy. We'd call a truce and just leave each other alone.

Running a vintage clothing boutique was not without its hazards. Like the aforementioned spider. Also, there were mice. That was what I got when I crawled around old places looking for treasures. Vintage clothing was my thing. When I spotted a circle skirt, a great pair of pedal pushers, or a fabulous pair of wedge heels, my heart skipped a beat. It truly was an adrenaline rush. I'd turned my passion into a career when I opened It's Vintage Y'all, my little boutique in the charming small town of Sugar Creek, Georgia.

Today I wore a 1950s Ruth Starling flower-patterned dress. It had tiny rhinestone buttons down the front, with a full skirt and a darted waist-line. Perfect for spring, the dress was the bee's knees. On my feet, I wore pale yellow wedge heels with a small bow across the vamp. Wedges were my favorite, and the color brought out the buttery gerbera daisies in the dress.

I'd responded to an ad announcing vintage clothing for sale. That was what had led me to this old attic. At least there was a small window on the other side of the room. It allowed a tiny amount of daylight to seep into the room. It was a typical attic, with exposed beams, cobwebs, and stacks of boxes. An old dress form was in the corner by the window. Every time I peered up, I thought the thing was a person staring at me. Maybe that explained the creepy feeling I had right now.

I'd been told there were quite a few great vin-tage pieces in the old trunk that was located in the middle of this cramped space. Mostly, I was look-ing for hats right now. The woman who had placed the ad had found the items when she'd bought the house, and she said I could just take whatever I wanted. The words were like magic to my ears. I was willing to deal with almost anything for free vintage, even fighting a bear . . . or a bear-sized spider.

The trunk groaned as I opened the lid. Layers of dust whirled to life. My eyes widened when I spotted the red 1940s boater hat. The tilted hat had a narrow brim with a small red veil. Perched on the edge of the brim was a velvet flocked bird with feathers in matching red hues. I was in hat heaven. As I sifted through the trunk, I found many more. There must have been at least twenty hats—all equally fabulous.

Insects, mice, dust, and a few vintage items weren't all that I found in the attic. When I looked up from the old trunk, I gasped and fell back onto my butt. A woman was standing in the corner of the room. Her stare was locked on me. The sixtysomething woman wore a black, silk crepe, mid-length dress. On her hands were delicate white gloves. Discreet pearl drops dotted her ears, and a matching necklace adorned her neck. Her 1940s tilt hat was made of black cellophane straw. The crown of the hat was encircled with black grosgrain ribbon. She completed her outfit with simple black pumps and a matching pocketbook.

I found it odd that her hat looked so much like the ones in the trunk. Had she taken one of the hats? I hadn't heard her enter the room. Maybe I'd been so consumed by the hat that I hadn't noticed. Had she been here all along? Once I was finally on my feet again, I stood in front of the trunk, with several hats still in my arms. Since the woman's frown sent a clear message that she wasn't happy to see me, I used the trunk as a shield. It created a nice barrier between us.

"What do you think you're doing?" she demanded.

"Cookie Chanel, come down from there. I'm not coming in. I don't want to get my outfit dirty. Besides, I may be a ghost, but I'm not joining you in that spooky place."

Now was not the time to deal with Charlotte Meadows. She was a ghost who refused to leave my side. Ever since I'd found her at an estate sale, she'd been stuck to me like flies on honey. She'd been attached to her killer wardrobe, but now she was affixed to me.

I looked at the corner again. The attic ghost wasn't there. "Where'd you go?"

I looked to the other side of the room. Now she was there. Was she playing games with me?

I focused my attention on her so she couldn't get away. "I'm sorry, but the woman downstairs said these hats were available."

She shifted the pocketbook from her right arm to her left. "They're my hats, and they're not available."

This was a bummer. As I put the hats back in the trunk, I noticed something odd. The lower half of the woman was completely see-through. Why hadn't I noticed that sooner? The longer I looked at her, the more solid she became. Unfortunately, I knew exactly what this meant. Oh no, not again. Why was this happening to me? I enjoyed helping ghosts, but I was just confused . . . why me?

I had to let this woman know that she was no longer in this dimension. Were the hats in the trunk hers? Considering the gorgeous hat she wore, I'd be willing to bet that was the case. I could understand why she was so concerned about the ones in the trunk. I picked the hats up again. A ghost wouldn't keep me from taking them.

"You do realize that you are a ghost?" I asked as I filled my arms with the hats.

She glared at me. "Well, that's neither here nor there. They're my hats."

So she did know she was a ghost.

Charlotte poked her head through the door. Literally. "What seems to be the problem, Cookie? Hurry it up. I don't want to have to come all the way in there."

Before I could answer, Charlotte spotted the woman across the room. Suddenly, Charlotte had no problem with setting foot in the attic. She popped in and stood beside me with her arms crossed in front of her chest. Charlotte was pretty territorial about me, as if I was her own personal psychic. Charlotte was dressed in a white tailored pantsuit. A beige silk tank top peeked out from under her jacket. On her feet, she wore five-inch heels and nude-colored Christian Louboutins. That was one perk of being a spirit: Charlotte got to wear whatever outfit she thought up in her mind.

Charlotte tapped her foot against the floor. "And who is this?"

"Not that it's any of your concern, but my name is Maureen Weber." She stared at Charlotte. "Who are you?"

"I'm Charlotte Meadows. That's all you need to know."

I could see this was getting nowhere.

"Maureen, I understand you're attached to your hats, but since you no longer need them, maybe I could let someone else use them who would really enjoy them." I forced a huge smile.

"So you want to steal my hats."

Charlotte shook her fist. "Don't call Cookie a thief."

I clapped my hands. "Ladies, ladies, let's not argue, shall we?"

What could I do to get this woman to let me have the hats? I supposed I would just have to leave them in the trunk. It was sad, really, because I was on a mission to find fantastic hats for a very special event. Danielle Elston had requested vintage hats to wear for the upcoming Kentucky Derby. She simply couldn't go to the Derby without a fantastic hat. Danielle had the money to buy any new hat she wanted, but she had requested that I help her.

Maureen moved a couple steps closer. She was totally solid now.

"I know she's a ghost." Maureen pointed at Charlotte. "But there's something different about you. I think you're still with the living." Maureen sashayed over to us.

Charlotte rolled her eyes. "Good heavens. It looks like two pigs fighting in a sack. One says you let me go by this time and I'll let you go by the next."

"Charlotte! That's not very nice," I said.

Maureen looked me up and down. "How can you see me if you're the living?"

I exchanged a look with Charlotte. "I don't really know how I can see you."

A huge smile spread on Maureen's face. "Since you can see me, you can help find my murderer."

Chapter 2

Cookie's Savvy Tips for Vintage Shopping

*Often vintage clothing can be purchased
for a fraction of the cost of buying new.*

My bags were all packed and loaded into the trunk of my car. It was a good thing I had plenty of room back there. I might have gone a little overboard with the luggage. It was almost impossible to pick just a few outfits to take though. I had no idea how many events I would attend. And a girl had to be stylish. The excitement was all just too much. Danielle insisted I come to the Derby to make sure her outfits were always spot-on.

I had said good-bye to my best friend, Heather, and my mother. They would be watching the shop until I got back.

I'd decided to drive to Kentucky. A car like mine would make the trip even more enjoyable.

My grandfather had left me his mint-condition red 1946 Buick convertible. It was an eye-catcher. Plus, since I was driving, I could easily take Wind Song with me. The gorgeous white feline had mysteriously shown up at my doorstep. Her sudden appearance wasn't the only thing mysterious about her either. I'd quickly discovered that she could use tarot cards and a Ouija board. I know that sounds crazy, but there is an explanation.

"Why not leave the cat—er, I mean Grandma Pearl—here?" Heather had asked. "She can stay with us at the shop."

I rubbed Wind Song's head. "Because Grandma Pearl always wanted to go to the Derby."

Yes, my grandmother had slipped into the cat's body during a séance. Now I had to figure out how to get her out of there, though I was almost sure she didn't want to leave.

I loaded up the car and placed Wind Song in the driver's seat.

"She will just have to share the seat with me," Charlotte said from the passenger seat.

Wind Song hissed at Charlotte.

"Please tell your grandmother not to talk to me that way." Charlotte sat up straight in the seat.

"Maybe I will reconsider this whole trip if you two plan on bickering the whole ride," I said, shoving the key into the ignition.

Charlotte had become a dear friend, but she

really knew how to push everyone's buttons at times.

"Okay, I promise not to argue with your grandmother, who is now a cat."

"Thank you for not arguing with my grandmother the cat," I said.

If anyone heard what I'd said, they would think I'd lost my mind.

There was no way Charlotte was going to stay behind while I went to the Derby. She had already modeled her hat for me. Since Charlotte was a ghost, all she had to do was think of the outfit she wanted to wear and—poof—it would appear.

I had spent quite a bit of time looking for my hat, though now I felt like I had found the perfect one for the first Saturday in May. It was white with a black ribbon around the brim and red flowers on the side. I'd recently picked it up for a fantastic price at an estate sale.

Maureen was sitting in the middle of the backseat. She shook her head. "It's like I'm riding to Kentucky with the three stooges. Except one of the stooges is a cat."

"Are you insulting us?" Charlotte asked.

I frowned as I looked in the rearview mirror. "That's not nice, Maureen."

"Sometimes the truth hurts," she said.

I wasn't sure how this trip was going to turn out when I had two ghosts along for the ride.

Finally, we hit the Kentucky state line. It was rolling hills and green grass for as far as I could see. Maureen was a socialite like Charlotte. Now I had two high-maintenance ghosts hanging around. As if one wasn't enough, now I had two ghosts competing for my attention.

Wind Song had mysteriously appeared at my shop. Turns out it was really my dearly departed Grandmother Pearl. That explained why the cat could read tarot cards and use a Ouija board.

Derby Week would be jam-packed with activities. Wind Song would enjoy seeing the horses and the fashions. I was staying at a charming old bed-and-breakfast. At least that was the way it had looked from the photos. Now I just needed to find the place. The photos of Woodhaven Inn had shown a lovely wide front porch where I could relax and enjoy a glass of iced tea. I was looking forward to that. Leafy maple trees surrounded the historic home, providing ample shade. Pink blossoms popped up around the lawn like bridesmaids' bouquets.

Chapter 3

Grandma Pearl's Pearls of Wisdom

Mind your own biscuits and life will be gravy.

"I think you're going the wrong way," Charlotte yelled as she pointed toward the exit sign.

I cut the wheel and sped down the exit ramp.

"You're going to kill us all over again," Maureen said.

Wind Song meowed.

"I've got everything under control. Don't worry. Plus, you two are already dead. I'm positive that I can't kill you again. And cats have nine lives, right?" I said with a chuckle.

Charlotte, Maureen, and Wind Song glared at me.

"Tough crowd," I said.

The bed-and-breakfast was on the outskirts of town and about a thirty-minute drive from Churchill Downs. Yet it felt as if I was in the country. The old house was surrounded by oak, pine, and magnolia trees. It was a red-brick federal-style home. A large porch with white columns welcomed me to the front door. Black urns with big ferns were spaced out along the length of the porch. I walked up the steps and rang the doorbell. Glancing over my shoulder as I waited for someone to answer, I couldn't help but notice just how dark it was out here.

"This place is spooky," Charlotte said, rubbing her arms and acting as if she had a shiver. "I bet it's haunted."

I stared at her.

"What? Just because I'm a ghost doesn't mean I'm not afraid of ghosts. Remember?"

I'd never understand Charlotte.

After what seemed like forever, someone opened the door. The gray-haired woman smiled at me. She wore a sweatshirt with tiny pictures of cats on the front. Brown pants coordinated her outfit. Definitely not vintage.

"Good evening. You must be Ms. Chanel," she said.

"Yes, please call me Cookie."

"I'm Hannah Olson, the proprietor. Come on in, and I'll show you to your room." She motioned for me to come inside.

"Well, at least she seems nice enough," Charlotte said.

Charlotte hardly paid anyone a compliment that quickly. Preparing to follow the woman through the house, I picked up one of my pieces of luggage with one hand and the cat carrier with the other.

Hannah immediately stopped and looked at the carrier. "What is that?"

"My cat. You said it wasn't a problem to bring her along."

"I said that?" She frowned.

"Yes, I'm sure it was you when I booked the room." I held the carrier up so she could get a better look at how pretty Wind Song was.

Charlotte eyed Hannah up and down. "Does she not like cats? She's wearing a cat sweatshirt, for heaven's sake."

Hannah slumped her shoulders as if the weight of the world was now on her. "I suppose that would be okay."

Her reaction was a bit dramatic, in my opinion.

"Do you have a cat?" I asked.

"No, why?"

My gaze traveled down to her sweatshirt. "No reason."

"If you'd like, I can show you around tomorrow and tell you the history of the house. I suppose you'd rather wait since it's getting so late this evening." She looked at the grandfather clock with a frown.

"That means you came too late, and she doesn't want to show you tonight," Charlotte said.

Yes, I got the hint.

"That would be nice. Thank you," I said.

The woman took me upstairs and down the hall. The bannister squeaked as I grabbed hold. Under my feet, the treads on the stairs moaned with each step. Dim light made it difficult to see exactly where I was going. Cream and gold wallpaper with a scroll and floral pattern covered the walls that led from the first to the second floor.

"Are the floors original to the house?" I asked when we reached the top of the staircase.

"Of course. And I've completely restored the house."

"It's lovely," I said as I took in the rich wood molding and trim.

She opened the door. "Well, here it is. I think you'll love this room. If you need anything, just let me know. Breakfast will be ready at seven in the morning."

I would have to set my alarm if I wanted to be awake that early.

"Thank you," I said.

She eyed me up and down. "See you then."

I placed my bags down and collapsed onto the bed. Charlotte and Maureen were checking out the room. Wind Song was busy sniffing around too. The room had floral wallpaper as well. The cream background made the soft greens and blues of the flowers pop. A cherrywood four-poster bed was pushed against the wall in the middle of the room. Two blue upholstered chairs and a small table made a conversation area on the far wall in front of the window.

"I hope we don't see any ghosts tonight," Charlotte said, peeking into the closet. "Maureen, I don't understand why you're here. Save yourself. You don't have to be here."

"Um, Charlotte, in case you have forgotten, you

don't have to be here either." I adjusted the pillow under my head.

She turned to face me and placed her hands on her hips. "I have got to take care of you. No one else is going to be here to do it."

I groaned and placed the pillow over my head to drown out their conversation. How would I get any sleep if they kept talking?

After a few more minutes, I stumbled out of bed. "I'm slipping into my pajamas. Can't you two go haunt the rest of the house?"

"Come on, Maureen. Let's check out our surroundings." Charlotte motioned over her shoulder.

Maureen followed Charlotte out the door.

Thank goodness. Now maybe I could get some sleep. I'd just finished brushing my teeth when my cell phone rang.

"Cookie, did you make it to town?" Danielle asked.

Danielle Elston had hired me to style her vintage fashion for the Derby, and I was determined to wow her with my flair.

"Yes, I'm here."

"Good. We have a luncheon in the morning. I need you to come by and help me decide what to wear."

After jotting down the address of the hotel where she was staying, I clicked off the phone and climbed into the four-poster bed. It had been a long day, and I had another long one ahead tomorrow. I needed rest so that I would be able to keep up with the fashion emergencies.

Wind Song was curled up beside me. I closed my eyes and tried to fall asleep, but I felt a presence. It was as if someone was watching me. The scent of gardenias tickled my nose.

I opened one eye and jumped. "Oh, Maureen, you scared me."

She'd been standing close to the bed, staring down at me.

"Is everything okay?" I asked as I sat up.

She sat on the side of the bed. "Cookie, I need you to find my killer."

"I told you I'd try my best." I yawned, not able to stop myself.

"It's just that you're so busy." She twisted her hands together.

"I'll call my mother and Heather. I'm sure they could look into things a little bit while I'm gone."

"Do you think they'll really be able to help?" Maureen asked with hope in her voice.

"Yes, of course they'll be able to help."

Honestly, I had no idea. But I was willing to stretch the truth a little if that would comfort her tonight.

"What about asking the detective you know to help? Charlotte said he's nice."

"He is nice, but I'm not sure I could ask him."

She sighed loudly. "It's okay. I'm just so worried. Would you stay up all night and comfort me?"

I quirked an eyebrow. Had she been talking to Charlotte about ways to annoy me?

"I suppose I can ask Dylan to help me."

She smiled. "That's wonderful. Thank you. Well, I guess I'd better let you get some sleep."

How easily she felt better. At least now I would get some sleep.

———

Chapter 4

Cookie's Savvy Tips for Vintage Shopping

> *Don't be afraid to buy something*
> *just because it doesn't have a brand label.*
> *If you love it, that's all that matters.*

I had no idea the charity luncheon would be such a star-studded event. I had never attended anything this fancy before. My red and white Evan Picone polka-dot dress fit just right, hugging my curves. The bust had a fun twist in the fabric, and the waist flared out at the bottom into the full skirt. My heels were four inches high, and instead of a hat, I wore a giant red flower in my hair. The flower was so large that it looked like a hat.

It was a good thing I had arrived early because Danielle wanted to try on quite a few outfits before finally deciding on a 1950s Christian Dior mint-colored dress with tiny white flowers throughout the fabric, which was perfect for the spring event. It had a large collar with an open neckline and a fitted waist. She wore a large white Lilly Daché hat with a mint-colored underside and a mint ribbon around the crown. Her white Dior clutch purse matched perfectly.

The event was being held inside the Kentucky Derby Museum at Churchill Downs. The building was adjacent to the track. Red and yellow tulips lined the path to the entrance. Danielle was getting the VIP treatment, and that meant I was too. That was something I was definitely not used to; I'd never gotten special treatment in the past.

White cloth-draped tables and white chairs were set up throughout the room. Chatter from the guests filled the air, and dishes clanked as everyone enjoyed a lunch of fried green tomatoes, country ham salad, grilled chicken, savory bread pudding, and cheese grits. After eating, Danielle and I were standing around watching the party-goers. Of course, the ghosts stood behind us. Danielle was pointing out celebrities.

"Is that Kim Kardashian?" Charlotte waved her hands as if that would get her noticed.

"Kim who?" Maureen asked.

Danielle pointed to someone else, taking my attention away from the ghosts. "I think he's on that reality show."

"Which one?" I asked, scanning the room.

"The guy or the reality show?" she asked.

I chuckled. "Both, I guess."

"You don't watch much television, do you?" she said.

"No, not really. I'm always running the shop, so

I miss a lot of it. I watch a lot of *I Love Lucy* reruns," I said with a smile.

As I sipped on my iced tea, I couldn't shake the sensation that someone was watching me. When I glanced around the room, I spotted a woman with long, blond hair staring at me. She wore a long, tight, black strapless dress, which was kind of odd since everyone else wore springlike colors— pinks and yellows and greens. I didn't recognize the designer of the dress. That always bugged me because I prided myself on knowing designers. I suppose I couldn't know all of them. She sipped on her drink but continued to stare. The fact that I was now watching her didn't deter her.

"Do you know that woman?" I leaned over and whispered into Danielle's ear.

"Which woman?" Danielle asked.

"The one over there . . . she's gone now."

"What did she look like?"

"Long, blond hair . . ."

A tall, black-haired man walked up and interrupted our conversation.

"That was just plain rude," Charlotte crossed her arms in front of her chest and tapped her foot against the floor. "He could have waited until you'd finished your conversation with Danielle before interrupting."

"I'll be right back, Cookie," Danielle said, getting up and walking away with the man.

Now I was all alone. Well, the ghosts were with me too, but no one else could see that I'd brought special guests. It was a good thing though, because the crowd would probably have run away. If the ghosts had been visible, they would have fit right in. Okay, Charlotte would have fit in. Maureen, not as much. Charlotte was wearing a strapless Christina Dior ruby-colored silk gown with a boned bodice. Her matching heels were Gucci. I was pleased to see Maureen in vintage, although she was slightly underdressed for the occasion. She wore a 1980s brown and white botanical print dress. With an empire waist and flowy sleeves, the dress looked like it was made in the 1940s. Her brown leather pumps were from Nine West. We needed to have a serious discussion about Maureen's fashion sense. One thing was for sure: Charlotte and Maureen were having a great time gossiping about the celebrities.

"I could really get used to this," Charlotte said.

Charlotte had been to many fancy events when she was alive, but I didn't think even she had been to something this extravagant. Since Danielle was busy talking to that tall man, I decided to visit the ladies' room to freshen my makeup. Danielle seemed to have slipped out to another part of the building, probably so it would be quieter and they could talk.

"You'd think they would offer a little more food than that for the price it cost to get into this place," Charlotte said.

"How do you know how much it cost to get in?" I whispered as we walked down the hallway.

It was a good thing I was alone out there. Now I could talk with Charlotte and Maureen. Well, I could answer back. They had been talking to me nonstop the whole time.

"I looked at someone's ticket who was sitting at the table across from us."

"You shouldn't spy on people," I said.

"It's not spying, darling. I mean, if they could see me, I'd do the same thing."

Charlotte strolled ahead of me toward the ladies' room.

She had a point. I knew she would do the same thing even if they could see her.

Maureen walked beside me. "Charlotte is sassy, isn't she?"

"You're telling me. I've been dealing with her for quite some time now."

"No offense, but I hope I don't have to stay around for too long," Maureen said.

"No offense taken," I said.

We reached the hallway that led to the restrooms. When I turned the corner, I spotted a body on the floor. Charlotte was standing over the man, peering down at him.

"Charlotte, what are you doing?" I ran down the hall.

"I think this guy's dead," she said.

Chapter 5

Grandma Pearl's Pearls of Wisdom

Hairstyles. The bigger, the better.

I rushed over to the man lying on the floor. He was near the men's room. He was small in stature, probably my height of five foot two. The man wore a light brown suit, a shade lighter than his hair.

"Sir, are you okay?" I called out in a panic.

"I'm telling you he's not okay, Cookie. He's dead," Charlotte said with a wave of her hand.

"Dead as a doornail," Maureen offered.

"You two aren't making this any better," I said. "What should I do?"

"We're just telling it like we see it. Right, Maureen?" Charlotte said.

Maureen moved closer to Charlotte, as if they formed a team now. "That's right."

Of course, the man didn't answer. He was lying

in an awkward position That was definitely not natural or comfortable. I reached down to check his pulse.

"He's dead," I said when I leaned up.

"I tried to tell you," Charlotte said.

Panic surged through me. I had to get help for this man. Maybe it wasn't too late to save him.

"Should I do CPR?" I asked as I pulled out my cell phone and dialed 911.

"Do you know how?" Maureen asked.

"Of course, she doesn't know how. I told her she should take a class. With the luck she has, it would come in handy. And see, I was right." Charlotte shook her head.

"Now is not the time for a lecture," I warned.

"This is nine one one. What's your emergency?" the female operator asked.

"There's a dead man here," I blurted out.

After I gave her the address, she helped me attempt CPR. I had no idea what I was doing. I worried I'd do more harm, but even though he was already dead, I felt I had to do something. I did as I was told, but nothing was happening. Charlotte and Maureen were pacing. I couldn't believe no other people had come into the restroom area. I could use a little help.

Thank goodness, soon sirens sounded, and I knew help was right outside. Within seconds, the police had descended on the area. There was nothing more I could do now. I backed away and let them handle it.

"You did a good job," Charlotte said.

"Yes, good work, Cookie," Maureen said. "There was nothing you could do. He was a goner." Maureen made a gesture with her index finger across her throat.

"I wonder what happened to him," I whispered.

"Cookie, are you okay?" Danielle called out.

I turned to see her running down the hallway toward me. Now she came. I could have used her a few minutes ago.

"I heard the sirens, and someone said it was you."

"I found this man." I gestured toward the area. "I'm pretty sure he's dead."

Danielle craned her neck to the side for a better view of the body. Police were blocking the view. Other guests were trying to get a glimpse of the action too.

She gasped. "Oh! Do you know who that is?"

"No, who is it?" I asked.

"He's the jockey who was going to ride our horse in the Derby."

"Oh, that's terrible," I said.

"Bummer," Maureen said.

"What happened to him?" Danielle asked.

I shrugged. "I don't know. I came down the hallway, and he was just lying on the floor."

"His name is Ramon Gooden."

"I'm so sorry," I said, giving her a hug.

"I have to make a call," she said with panic in her voice.

Danielle disappeared down the hallway. There

were quite a few people standing around. They were whispering and looking at me too. This was awkward. I hoped that I'd be able to slip out of there soon. Finding a dead body was a traumatic experience.

Most people had been allowed to leave, but I had to stay around to be questioned by the police. Maureen and Charlotte were becoming bored.

"When do we get to leave?" Charlotte paced across the floor.

Danielle was waiting around with me. The police had talked with her, but they didn't have nearly as many questions for her as they did for me. I wished that Detective Dylan Valentine was here. He worked for the Sugar Creek Police Department back home in Georgia. We'd grown quite close recently. This made Charlotte extremely happy though she liked my friend attorney Ken Harrison too.

As I stood by the door waiting for the police to tell me I could leave, I spotted something on the ground. It had fallen behind the fake potted plant. I was surprised the police hadn't seen it. The gold, shiny object looked like a bracelet. I looked around to see if anyone else had noticed it.

"Leave it to you to find the fashion item," Charlotte said.

I inched over closer to the spot. When I felt no one was watching, I leaned down and picked up the item. Was this considered evidence? Should I have really touched it? I didn't know if this even had anything to do with the murder. The thing had probably rolled under there when someone dropped it. I had seen this bracelet before. Well, not this exact one per se, but I knew the designer. Cartier started making this particular style of bracelet in the 1970s. It was still as popular today as it had been in the past. The style hadn't changed either.

"Oh, Cartier." Charlotte pursed her lips. "Nice find."

"It is a classic," I said, staring at it a bit longer.

I shoved it in my pocket. I wasn't sure why I wasn't turning it in to the police, but I felt as if I had to research this. Maybe I would call Dylan and tell him about finding it, though he would probably tell me to give it to the police. Detective Anderson was apparently the lead detective investigating what had happened to Ramon. He had given me his card and said to call if I remembered any other details, so it wasn't like I didn't have a contact number. Nevertheless, revealing that I had discovered something at the scene of the crime would be a wait and see situation. Maybe I'd tell and maybe I wouldn't. The bracelet was expensive. But any number of people in this place could have afforded it. I felt bad for being sneaky, but it was something that I felt I had to do.

"I know what you're doing, Cookie," Charlotte said.

I looked down at my shoes so no one would see me talking. "What am I doing?"

"You don't want to give the bracelet to the police because you want to track down the owner yourself. You can't keep yourself away from a mystery."

Okay, so she was right about that, but was that so wrong? I was only trying to help.

"I am just trying to help."

"You can help by giving them the evidence." Charlotte placed her hands on her hips. "Now give it to that officer."

I didn't budge.

"Cookie Chanel, you give that bracelet to the police right this minute. They will think you're stealing it."

Why was she always right? I walked over to the officer standing by the exit door and handed him the bracelet.

"He'll probably keep it," I mumbled.

"That's not nice. You stop being sassy. What's gotten into you lately?"

I didn't need to be scolded.

"Hey, you," someone whispered from over my shoulder.

I gasped.

"Oh, don't do that," Charlotte clutched her chest. "You scared me."

She was scared? How did she think I felt? I was startled too when I saw the dead jockey standing behind me. I stared at him, unable to speak.

"Can you tell me what's going on around here? Am I dead?"

"Oh, another one," Charlotte said.

Yes, that was exactly my thought. Telling someone that they were dead was never easy.

"Yes, I'm afraid you have passed on to the next dimension." I said with a wave of my arm, as if showing him the exit door.

Eternity is right through that door, sir. Please watch your step on the way out.

"He hasn't gone anywhere," Charlotte said. "He's just dead, but not yet in the other dimension. He's still on this plane."

Charlotte seemed upset that another ghost was with us. At this point, what was one more? He couldn't be any more talkative than Charlotte and Maureen. My relaxing trip to Kentucky had certainly turned upside down.

"What happened to me?" Ramon asked.

"All signs point to murder," Charlotte said matter-of-factly.

Chapter 6

Cookie's Savvy Tips for Vintage Shopping

Don't be afraid to try new things.
Just because the style isn't current
doesn't mean you can't wear it.

I was back at the bed-and-breakfast. Needless
to say, I was stunned by the turn of events. I was
even more shocked when I realized that the ghost
of the dead jockey had followed me back to the
bed-and-breakfast. He knew he'd been murdered,
and now he needed me to find his killer. How
could I possibly do that? I was in a new town and
knew hardly anyone. Scratch that, I knew no one
here.

Hannah Olson, my landlady, had tapped her
foot against the hardwood floor and placed her
arms in front of her chest. Based on the glare she
gave me, I knew she didn't appreciate that I was
late coming back. She also didn't appreciate that

I'd told her about being involved in a murder investigation.

"I don't know what kind of shady business you're involved in, but I don't want you bringing that stuff back here." She stomped off.

"I'll haunt her tonight," Charlotte said.

"Oh no! Don't make things worse than they already are. The whole city of Louisville is booked for the Derby, and I'd never find another place to stay if she kicked me out."

What would be even worse was if the owner found out I'd brought back the ghost of the man who'd been murdered. Was there an extra charge for ghostly guests?

After feeding Wind Song, I slipped into my pajamas and applied my nightly face cream. I plopped down on the bed and closed my eyes. Hannah would probably prefer that I not lie on top of the white and pink floral-patterned duvet. I didn't have the energy to move anything off the bed. The dainty pink pillows were under my head.

"You can't go to sleep yet," Charlotte said. "You have to talk with Ramon first."

I opened one eye. "What's to talk about?"

"The fact that I was murdered." The wrinkle between Ramon's eyes deepened.

I sat up in bed. "So you think you were murdered for sure? Tell us what happened."

I didn't think he wanted to talk about it.

"I remember a strange feeling, as if I couldn't see clearly. Next thing I knew someone attacked me from behind. Then I was floating around looking at my lifeless body on the floor."

"That says to me murder," Charlotte said.

"I need you to find my killer," Ramon said.

"If anyone can do it, Cookie can," Charlotte said.

"Thanks for the vote of confidence, Charlotte. There's not enough time in the day to solve all the mysteries I seem to encounter. There's Maureen, did you forget about her?" I motioned. "She needs me to find out why she's hanging around."

Maureen stepped forward. "I can wait if Ramon needs help first. I'm in no hurry . . ."

I held up my hand to stop Maureen from finishing her sentence. "Of course, you're in a hurry, Maureen. Don't be bashful about asking for my help." I had already promised her my time.

Ramon flashed a sad look my way. "I guess I'll just hang around with you and wait. You have to find my killer."

"The only clue at the scene was a bracelet," Charlotte said. "It could be the killer's. Who would have owned the Cartier bracelet?"

I waved my hand. "I'm not sure if I could find that out."

"Just harass her. She'll eventually give in and do it." Charlotte leaned against the dresser.

"I'm not as easily manipulated as you think."

"She hates it when you wake her up singing. Oh, and pop in on her when she's in the shower too. That makes her testy."

Ramon's eyes widened.

"Don't you dare," I warned.

I'd told him I couldn't do it, but I knew I would. It wouldn't be easy though. I didn't even know where to start. I suppose I'd find a way. Ramon looked at me with his big brown eyes.

I sighed. "Okay, I'll do it."

Charlotte tossed her hands up.

"What?" I asked.

"I can't believe you gave in so easily. It took me forever to convince her."

I propped my hands behind my head and smiled. Yes, it gave me a little bit of satisfaction to ruffle Charlotte's feathers. She'd been doing it to me for quite a while, and now it was payback time.

As soon as Wind Song, aka Grandma Pearl, spotted Ramon's ghost, she rushed over to him. She weaved around his legs and meowed.

"I think the cat likes you, Ramon," Charlotte said.

"She doesn't usually take to people that quickly," I said. "Although Grandma Pearl seemed to like Dylan awfully quickly."

"Who can blame her for that?" Charlotte said. "I liked him quickly too."

I sat down on the bed with my laptop. Just because I wasn't at home in Sugar Creek didn't mean that I wasn't going to blog. I planned to post throughout my entire experience visiting the Derby. I would have a lot to talk about. I had just started typing when Wind Song came over and sat beside me. She stared down at the keyboard, and the next thing I knew she was placing her paws on it.

"She wants to type a message," Charlotte said.

I moved my hands so that she could move her paws around to all the letters. It wasn't easy for her to use the keys. When she'd hit one key, three letters would appear. Her paws were too big. How would I ever make out this message? There were a few numbers and other symbols mixed in, though there were some letters. This was like a puzzle.

"I think she's spelled the word *poem*," Charlotte said.

"You could be right. Is that what you wanted to spell, Grandma Pearl?"

She meowed.

"I'd take that as a yes," Maureen said.

"I can't believe what I've gotten myself into," Ramon said. "A cat who types?"

"What do you think she means by *poem*?" Charlotte asked.

"I don't know, and it looks as if Wind Song is ready for a nap," I said.

Grandma had already closed her eyes and was lying on the pillow.

Chapter 7

Grandma Pearl's Pearls of Wisdom

Throw kindness around like confetti.

The next evening arrived, and I was dressing for the latest event. I wore a 1980s red Donna Karan gown with a draped cowl neckline and ruching through the bodice. My nude-colored Jimmy Choo heels, a faux-diamond necklace, and matching stud earrings finished the look.

"Okay, you can come in now," I called out to the ghosts.

Instantly, they popped into the room. Ramon whistled.

"Cookie, you look gorgeous," Maureen said.

"I'm still upset that you didn't wear the blue dress, but this one does look great." Charlotte winked.

"Thank you, everyone. I'm glad you like it."

I picked up my bag and checked my makeup one last time.

"You'd better hurry. You don't want to be late." Charlotte motioned for me to hurry.

I was attending an exclusive charity event tonight. Celebrities and other influential people would be in attendance, as well as people who Ramon thought might have clues as to who was responsible for his death. Also, I was supposed to meet the other people who worked with Danielle. I was never good with crowds. I never said the right thing or acted cool.

I'd helped select the dress and jewelry for Danielle. I hoped she was happy with what I'd picked out. She'd been busy, and I hadn't had a chance to talk with her since I had dropped off the dress at her hotel. I was always nervous when I picked out stuff for others. What if she wasn't wearing the dress and had opted for something else instead? Maybe she'd tell me she didn't need my help any longer.

I hugged Wind Song. "We'll be back soon, Grandma. Sorry we can't take you with us."

If I knew her, she was probably thinking, "Oh sure, take the ghosts, but not a cat."

"This event will be great," Ramon said. "We can talk with a lot of people who might have clues about who would want me dead."

I hurried down the hallway. "You think they will talk to me about you? They don't even know me."

"You'll figure out a way," Charlotte said.

The bed-and-breakfast owner was by the front door when I reached the foyer.

"Good evening. I suppose I will have to let you in at a late hour again this evening." The scowl on her face let me know she wasn't happy about this prospect.

"I should be back by eleven," I said.

"Eleven? Even Cinderella stayed out past midnight," Charlotte said.

The woman sighed and said, "I suppose I'll have to wait up. I guess I can watch the eleven o'clock news since I know you'll be late."

I forced a smile and headed out the door.

"I wouldn't leave her a good review on Yelp," Charlotte said.

Once outside, I weaved around the rosebushes, down the walking path, and reached my Buick. I pulled away from the house and drove along the winding, narrow road. The red and orange rays of the setting sun eclipsed the blue sky. Darkness was quickly moving in. I wished Dylan had been able to attend this event with me.

After getting lost a couple of times on the winding roads of a massive local park, I located the street where the party was being held. The mansions were on the outer edges of the park. My destination stood out because a large crowd had gathered to get a glimpse of the celebrities. I pulled up to the parking area and showed my invitation and my identification.

After getting out of the car, I headed toward the house. I was nervous about going into the party alone. I wished Danielle could have met me outside. Most celebrities were arriving by limousine. The crowd cheered when someone stepped out from the back of a dark car. I couldn't see who was in the latest one though. Somehow, I ended up walking the red carpet at the same time as this celebrity.

Once inside the mansion, I stood by the door, trying to take it all in and also trying to hide. There was so much to look at, including the stunning house and all the celebrities. Crystal chandeliers lit every room. Marble and hardwood floors and extensive moldings reminded me of Charlotte's house.

"Stop gawking," Charlotte said. "Try to act natural, like you belong here."

"I don't think I belong here," I whispered.

"Why do you say that?" Maureen asked.

"I don't like this kind of stuff. It's too much for me. I like things less glitzy."

"Oh, please, you love glamour," Charlotte said.

"Yes, quiet glamour."

"I don't even know what that means," Charlotte said.

"Oh, look, it's Jon Voight," Charlotte said as she walked away.

This probably wouldn't end well for the actor. When I peered across the crowd, Charlotte was already standing beside him. She touched his arm, and he looked around as if he'd felt a breeze. Bringing the ghosts here was probably a bad idea, but it wasn't like I'd had a choice. I looked out over

the crowd again. Was that Richie Sambora and
Megyn Kelly talking? I didn't like being here
alone at all. If I didn't spot Danielle soon, I was
just going to leave. I'd much rather be back at my
room reading a book . . . in my own quiet, private
world. Well, private with three ghosts and a cat
that was actually my grandmother.

"Glad you made it," a woman said from over
my shoulder.

When I turned around, Danielle was standing
behind me. Another woman was with her. It was
the woman from the earlier event, the one who'd
been staring at me. Now I realized that maybe
she'd been staring at Danielle. The woman looked
my way again. Her dark brown eyes seemed as if
they could stare a hole right through you.

Danielle looked at my dress. "You look great."

I was afraid to mention her dress for fear that
she would tell me how much she hated it.

"Thank you, and that dress looks fantastic on
you," I said.

She smiled. "I absolutely love it. I've gotten a
lot of compliments on it."

Whew. That was a relief. Just a few more outfits
for her, and I'd be finished.

"Cookie, I'd like you to meet Mandy Neville."
Danielle gestured at the woman standing next
to her.

The woman stared at me as she took a sip of her
champagne. Chills tingled down my spine. I
should have attempted a handshake, but I knew
without trying that Mandy wouldn't want that.

"Nice to meet you," I said.

She gave me a halfhearted smile and said, "Nice to meet you too."

"That didn't sound genuine," Maureen said.

"She's a trainer," Ramon said. "She just takes some getting used to, that's all."

"Well, I don't like her." Charlotte had returned.

I could always count on Charlotte to give me her honest opinion.

"Danielle, can I talk to you for a moment?" Mandy gestured over her shoulder.

"Um, sure, we'll be right back, Cookie."

The women walked away.

"Apparently, Mandy didn't want you to hear what she had to say," Charlotte said. "Well, don't worry, I will go listen."

"Charlotte, I don't think you should do that." I pretended to wipe something off my dress while looking down so no one would be suspicious of me talking to myself.

I'd gotten clever with my ways of disguising my chats with the ghosts.

"Why not?" She frowned.

"Because they obviously wanted to have a private conversation."

Charlotte huffed. She knew I was right. When I gazed over at the women, they appeared to be in a bit of a heated conversation. Danielle moved her arms while she talked, and Mandy had her fists clenched by her sides. Were they actually going to throw punches soon? Mandy looked like she'd love to yank Danielle's pretty blond hair out of her updo.

"Just admit it. Now you really want to know what they're saying," Charlotte said.

Okay, I did want to know now. Maybe if I just eased over, I could pick up a few words.

"Are you Cookie?" the woman's voice said from behind me.

I spun around, almost spilling my champagne. A pretty, middle-aged brunette and an older bald man stood behind me.

"You're in trouble now, Cookie. They probably heard you talking and think you were talking to yourself," Charlotte said.

Well, who did I have to thank for that?

"Yes, I'm Cookie," I said with a smile, trying to act completely normal.

That was tough when I had three ghosts standing around chatting in my ear.

"I'm Elise Beebe, and this is Lewis Elston." She stuck out her hand.

I shook her hand. "Oh yes, you're a racing manager. Nice to meet you. And you own the horse." I shook Lewis's hand too.

He smiled and said, "Yes, I'm the lucky one."

"Are you having a nice time?" Elise asked.

"Yes, thank you for inviting me. So far, everything has been fantastic."

"Well, except for discovering the dead guy," Charlotte quipped.

Ramon reached for a champagne glass from a

nearby tray, but his hand went right through it. "Yes, there is that."

Elise noticed when I turned my attention toward Danielle and Mandy. It looked as if they were still in a heated exchange.

"Is everything all right with them?" Elise asked.

"I'm not sure," I said.

"Maybe we should find out what's going on," Lewis said.

"Nice to meet you, Cookie." Elise smiled.

They walked away.

Now I really wanted to move closer to hear what was being said.

But my plan soon changed when Ramon said, "What is she doing here?"

"Who?" I asked.

He lifted his arm and pointed across the room. "My wife."

Charlotte and I exchanged a look. "Your wife is here?"

Ramon didn't wait to answer. He took off across the room.

"Why would she come here so soon after his death? Shouldn't she be in mourning?" Maureen asked. "Wearing all black?"

"I suppose people handle things differently," I said.

"I still find it highly suspicious," Charlotte said. "Let's go see what she's doing."

Charlotte and Maureen took off across the room, and I had no choice but to make my way over there too. Okay, I had a choice, but I wanted to know what was going on too. I smiled at the people who looked at me strangely when I squeezed past them. Honestly, I never expected a house this big to be this jam-packed.

Finally, I reached the woman. She had flowing dark hair that reached the middle of her back. She wore a sexy, spaghetti-strap black dress with a double row of rhinestones all the way down the front of the fabric, which gathered in the front and had a long slit. She oozed glamour, which I assumed came effortlessly for her.

"Cookie, you need to talk to her. Her name is Kristina. Find out why she came here," Ramon said.

Clearly, Ramon was also upset that she was here.

"I'm trying to think of something to say." I covered my talking by pretending to take a sip from my glass of champagne. I'd never actually taken a drink of the bubbly yet. I'd been too busy talking to ghosts. My life was *so* not normal. How would I strike up a conversation with this stranger? What would I say? "Hey, I'm the one who found your dead husband?"

When I scanned the room, I noticed Mandy storm away from Danielle, Elise, and Lewis. Apparently, she was unhappy about something.

Chapter 8

Cookie's Savvy Tips for Vintage Shopping

Practice makes perfect.
The more you shop for vintage,
the better you'll get at identifying vintage.

Mandy moved over to the bar and ordered another martini. I watched as she scanned the crowd. It was clear from her tense posture and furrowed brow that she didn't want to be here.

"I wonder who she's looking for now?" Charlotte asked.

"There's just something about her that rubs me the wrong way," Maureen said.

"She does have that creepy vibe. Kind of like the black widow. I wouldn't turn my back on her, that's for sure," Charlotte said.

"She's okay," Ramon said. "You just have to get to know her."

"No thanks," Maureen and Charlotte said at the same time.

They were being awfully critical of a woman they didn't even know.

"Forget about Mandy right now," Ramon said. "I want you to talk with my wife."

"Oh, yeah. That. I suppose I should talk with her."

Maybe Kristina could provide some clue as to who may have wanted Ramon dead. She might be able to tell me about enemies that Ramon didn't even realize he had. Sometimes people don't realize that someone doesn't like them, but the people closest to them will pick up on it. Just as I moved closer to talk with Kristina, she walked away.

"Where is she going?" Charlotte asked.

It looked as if she was headed straight toward Mandy. After navigating the crowd, sure enough, Kristina stood in front of Mandy. Kristina placed her drink on the bar. That wasn't a good sign. It was as if she knew she'd need her hands free for this encounter. Mandy gave her a look that could kill.

"I want to know why you were having an affair with my husband." Kristina didn't try to lower her voice.

"Uh-oh," Charlotte said.

"This is better than a soap opera," Maureen said.

"It's like a real-life soap opera," Charlotte said.

When I glanced at Ramon, he was looking away. Kristina moved closer to Mandy.

"This is going to get good," Charlotte said.

"I bet they start throwing punches soon," Maureen said.

"Don't say that," Ramon said. "Do something to stop them, Cookie."

What did he want me to do? I certainly didn't want to jump in and get punched.

The next thing I knew, a punch was thrown. Kristina's fist missed Mandy's face by less than an inch. Kristina swung again, and this time she made contact. Mandy screamed and put her hand to her face. She looked shocked at the turn of events.

"Cookie, you have to stop the fight," Ramon said.

I held my hand up to my mouth and pretended to cough. "What do you want me to do? I'm not a boxer."

Luckily, I didn't have to step in because security was there in the blink of an eye. Two muscular men grabbed the women and pulled them away from each other.

Charlotte stepped back. "Cookie, move away so people don't think you're involved. They'll throw you out of the party too."

The women struggled with the security officers for a few seconds until the men finally escorted them through the door.

"You have to follow them. What if they continue the fight outside?" Ramon said.

"They're adults. They can handle it without Cookie. She doesn't need to be involved in a physical altercation," Charlotte said.

I had to agree with her on that. I did want to see

what happened to them next though. I moved through the crowd over to the door. People were still talking about what had happened, but things were getting back to normal now.

I looked at Ramon. "Did you really do that? Have an affair?"

"Who me?" Ramon didn't blink as he stared at me. "Of course not."

Security had talked with both women. After a few more tense seconds, Mandy walked away.

"Should we follow her?" Charlotte asked.

"I don't think so. What would we learn from that?"

"Maybe she'll make a phone call or something and talk about what happened at the party," Maureen said.

"I think we saw what happened at the party. Kristina thought Mandy was cheating with her husband, so she confronted her. That seems pretty straightforward."

"If you say so," Charlotte said.

Mumbling under her breath, Mandy stomped away. She never turned to look back at Kristina. Maybe she hadn't been ready to leave the party but was forced out, whether she wanted to go or not. Glittering stars peeked through fast-moving clouds. Chatter from the crowds lining the roped-off sections filled the night air. The entire event was nothing short of chaotic.

"You're not even supposed to be here," the security officer said to Kristina. "Leave now and we won't call the police."

"Hey, you can't talk to her that way," Ramon said to the officer.

"He can't hear you," I reminded him.

"Oh, yeah." Ramon stepped away. "Well, you tell him."

"I'm not telling him anything. I don't want bodily harm."

Kristina yanked her arm back and stomped away.

"I hope Mandy doesn't try to confront Kristina now that they're away from security. Maybe now we should go check it out." Ramon walked ahead a few steps.

I didn't want to be in the middle of their fight. Especially if punches were thrown.

I turned to Ramon. "You said you weren't having an affair with Mandy. I'm not sure if I believe you. No wonder your wife is upset. That's why she came here, to confront Mandy. She's obviously grieving and upset."

"I'm telling you I didn't have an affair with her." He peered down at his shiny black shoes.

Charlotte, Maureen, and I stared at him.

He held his arms up. "I promise I didn't. Mandy was the one trying to seduce me, but I refused her advances."

"Oh yeah, a pretty woman was seducing you. Couldn't she just find a single guy?" Charlotte asked.

"That's what I asked her, but she said she didn't want a single guy. It was much easier to date a married man."

"That's disgusting," Maureen said. "She should be ashamed."

"Something tells me she's not," Charlotte said.

"I think she uses men to get what she wants," Ramon said. "She's manipulative."

"You just said earlier that she took getting used to and that she was okay," I said.

"Well, I was just trying to be nice," he said.

"What did she want from you?" Charlotte asked.

Ramon shrugged. "I don't know."

There was something tense about his posture. I didn't think he was telling the truth.

I looked at my phone. "Oh no. it's getting late. I should get back to the bed-and-breakfast before I get in trouble."

"Cinderella has to get back before she turns into a pumpkin." Charlotte laughed.

I looked around for Danielle but didn't see her, so I decided to leave without saying good-bye.

"The party's just now starting," Maureen said.

I waved my hand as I made my way down the long drive toward the parking area. "There was nothing special going on anyway. Not for me at least. Maybe if I knew more people there."

I'd witnessed the argument between Kristina Gooden and Mandy. That was not what I'd expected to happen at the party. I still couldn't believe Kristina had accused Mandy of having an affair with her husband. I was shocked that Kristina had attended the party right after her husband's death. Apparently, she hadn't been invited but somehow had gotten in. I suppose that was just so that she could confront Mandy in public. I bet Kristina wanted everyone to know about their affair. Would Kristina really do that when she was grieving?

The noise from the event faded as I drove away. Sounds of traffic now replaced the chatter of human voices. The warmth of the day had disappeared, and a slight spring chill hung in the night air. I couldn't wait to get away from the city and back to the serenity of the bed-and-breakfast.

"If you had mingled, maybe you would have met some people."

"Oh well," I said.

Chapter 9

Grandma Pearl's Pearls of Wisdom

Pretty is as pretty does.

The next day, I had breakfast downstairs with Hannah. She was still upset because I'd been five minutes late. Maybe that explained why the pancakes were cold. I ate them anyway because I wasn't sure when I would get more food. With enough syrup on the stack, the pancakes weren't so bad. At least the fresh strawberries were good.

I had to be at the barn in an hour. Danielle wanted to show me around before we went shopping. She said there were a lot of great thrift stores in town, and I couldn't wait to take a look. After finishing the meal and thanking Hannah, I rushed upstairs so I could change clothes. I had no idea what I would wear today.

My outfit needed to be something casual so that I wouldn't worry about getting dirty. Not that I would be mucking barns or anything, but there was still a good chance I'd come in contact with some dirt. At least I hoped not to have to shovel stalls.

I decided on a pair of 1970s light blue Armani jeans. The legs had a slight flare. My pink 1950s linen blouse had a lace-embroidered high round neckline. My white Converse sneakers would have to do since that was all I had that was remotely close enough to comfortable for the occasion, though I knew there was little chance they would remain clean at the end of the day. I hopped in the car and took off toward Churchill Downs. This would be exciting. I'd never been before.

Wind Song had convinced me to take her too. She sat on the front seat of the car and wouldn't budge an inch for Charlotte. That was also Grandma's way of telling me I wasn't going without her. The white steeples became visible in the distance. I pulled up to the little wooden guard shack. A middle-aged man wearing a security uniform held up his hand for me to stop.

He stepped over to my window and asked, "Name, please?"

"Cookie Chanel," I said timidly.

After looking at his clipboard, he motioned me through. Churchill Downs was in a populated area, surrounded by houses and traffic. The fenced-in area at the back of the track held rows of white barns. People were walking some horses, while other horses peered out from their stalls. I pulled my car over to the parking area and hopped out.

"This is interesting," Charlotte said, as she peered down at the ground.

I knew she was watching to make sure she didn't step in anything the horses had left behind. Danielle said they were in barn number fourteen. After starting by walking the wrong way, I made a left and located the right number. I walked over to the area and stood by the entrance. Since I had no idea what I was doing there, I tried to stay out of the way.

It was still early for me, but it looked as if everyone around had been up and working for quite a while. The horses neighed as I inched closer. So far, I saw no one I recognized. I looked at my watch to make sure I had the correct time. Just as I turned around to head out, I spotted Elise in the office area as she talked on the phone. She hadn't seen me yet. I stepped over to wait for her to finish.

"It smells in here," Charlotte said as she waved her hand in front of her nose.

"Well, it is a barn," I whispered.

Eavesdropping wasn't my intention, but as I neared the door I couldn't help but overhear Elise talking. The topic of the conversation was Ramon.

"Well, I'm glad that I have another jockey riding the horse now. Ramon wouldn't do as I told him, so it was for the best."

My gaze fell on Ramon, who had heard the whole thing.

"I didn't have to do as she told me," he said with anger in his voice.

"Well, she is in charge of the horse," I whispered. "I think that means she gets to tell you how to ride the horse."

Ramon shook his head. "Not true."

"I have to win this race at all costs, and I wasn't going to let the jockey stand in my way," Elise said.

"I'm a good jockey," he said.

"Was . . . ," Charlotte corrected him.

"Just because I don't agree with her . . . She let the horse go out in the pasture and trained him a few days before the race," Ramon said.

"Isn't that what you're supposed to do?" I asked.

"She has a lot invested in the horse. Right now, she should just let him sit in the stall. What if he gets injured?" he asked.

"That's why you train them—so they won't get injured," I said. "It's like if I wanted to run a marathon. There's no way I could do it if I didn't train often. Train and then rest. Not all rest. No training would only cause me to have an injury because I wouldn't be physically fit to run," I said.

"How do you know so much about horses?" Charlotte asked.

I shrugged. "Just seems like common sense to me."

"I'm sorry. Were you talking to me?" Elise asked.

"Uh-oh," Maureen said.

I'd been so consumed with the ghostly conversation I'd forgotten that someone might hear me talking to myself. Sometimes I wished others could see the ghosts too.

"I was talking with the horse," I said with a chuckle.

Elise smiled. "He is beautiful, isn't he? Sorry. I was just on the phone." She motioned over her shoulder.

I knew she was feeling me out to see if I'd overheard her conversation. I didn't know whether to admit it or act as if I hadn't heard a thing.

"I just got here," I said.

Elise stared. "Well, would you like a tour?"

"Sure, that would be great."

Elise wore jeans and a T-shirt with the company's racing logo on the pocket. Her brown hair was pulled back into a ponytail, but a few stray hairs had escaped. Dark circles underlined her eyes.

"I can show you the track, if you'd like. There are probably horses there now."

"Danielle was supposed to meet me here," I said, scanning the area to see if Danielle was nearby.

"Danielle is always late, but I'm sure she will be here soon."

"You should go with her, Cookie," Maureen urged.

"I suppose I could go for a quick tour," I said.

"Cookie never does what I tell her that easily." Charlotte pouted.

Ramon glared at Elise. If looks could kill, she'd be joining him in ghostly form soon.

I still couldn't get over what Elise had said on the phone. Ramon knew that Elise was unhappy with him, so did he suspect Elise? Not wanting him to ride the horse was a big deal. And she hadn't hesitated to announce that she was happy a new jockey would be riding the champion thorough-bred. Elise said it herself: she wanted to win the race at all costs.

As we walked toward the track, I spotted Mandy. She was standing by one of the barns, talking to a dark-haired man. She pulled out her phone and took a selfie of the two of them.

"Who is she with?" I asked.

Elise looked over. "Oh, that's another famous trainer. Mandy loves to mingle and take selfies. She isn't much into actually training the horse."

"If she isn't doing the training, then who is?" I asked.

She smirked.

"Oh," I said. "So you do a lot around here?"

"Whatever needs to be done," she said. "Tech-nically I'm the racing manager, but I'm actually doing what Mandy is supposed to do. Of course, we have a fantastic horse groomer who takes care of the horse. To him the horses are like family."

"It's great to have so many wonderful people around the horse," I said.

We reached the black fence that separated the barn area from the track. Saddled horses with jockeys on their backs raced around the track.

"It's almost the big day. I've decided I'm retiring if I don't win this race. I just can't keep this up, so this is my last shot. I have to make this work."

"It seems as if she's willing to do anything to win," Charlotte said.

Even murder?

Elise's phone rang. "If you'll excuse me."

A horse was trotting by, so the noise was a bit loud.

When the sound faded, Ramon said, "I'm glad Elise is gone."

"I'm sure she didn't mean anything by what she said earlier," I said.

He leaned against the fence. "Never mind that. I just need you to do something for me."

"What's that?" I asked.

"We have to check out my locker."

"Oh, that's a good idea," Charlotte said with excitement.

Another horse galloped by. Ramon waited until it was gone so that I could hear him.

"The building is right over there." He pointed.

"The building marked 'private'? I can't go in there," I said.

"It won't take long. No one will see you. Everyone is either gone or on the track." Ramon gestured, urging me to go.

"Go on, Cookie, you should do it," Maureen said.

"It's a locker room. There will be men in there. Probably with no clothes on," I whispered.

"No, there are no jockeys in there right now." Ramon motioned for me to go ahead.

"What about Elise? She'll wonder where I went."

"You won't be gone that long," Charlotte said.

"She talks a long time on the phone. You'll have plenty of time," Ramon said.

The trio urged me to move forward.

I sighed and said, "Okay, but we have to move fast."

What was I saying? They always moved fast. I had to move fast. Plus, even if they were slow, no one would see them. After looking around, I rushed over to the building.

"Isn't it locked?" I asked.

"There's a push code to get in." He pointed at the door.

"Okay, what's the code?" I asked.

He tapped his chin with his index finger.

"Hurry," I said. "Can't you remember it? Didn't you go in there every day?"

"Okay, okay, it's four six five seven."

I punched in the numbers, and a little green light appeared.

"You're good to go now," Ramon said.

I pulled on the door, and it opened. "This is not right. I don't think I should be in here."

After peeking around to make sure I didn't spot any naked men, I inched into the room.

"There's nothing to see, Cookie. Don't worry," Charlotte said.

Not that I would trust her to tell me the truth. There was nothing she'd like more than to trick me into getting an eyeful.

"Which one is your locker?" I asked.

"It's right down that aisle." Ramon pointed.

"Please don't let anyone find me," I said under my breath as I headed that way.

After a couple of steps, Ramon said, "Wait. I was wrong; it's over there."

My heart thumped a little faster. I raced over to the next aisle.

"Which one?" I asked with panic in my voice.

Ramon held up his hand. "Wait. I guess it's on the other side."

I quirked an eyebrow.

"My bad," he said.

"Oh, you're just playing games with me now." I placed my hands on my hips.

"No, no, I'm not playing. It's over there. I'm just having a tough time remembering."

"Obviously," Charlotte said as she followed along.

I dashed over to the other aisle. "Now which one is it?"

Ramon counted down the lockers. "The sixth one down."

I counted the lockers and stopped in front when I reached the sixth one. "Okay, do you remember the code? They may have changed it already."

"Well, there's only one way to find out." Charlotte turned her attention to Ramon. "What's the code, Ramon?"

Ramon tapped his index finger against his bottom lip again. "Let's see. I always had a hard time remembering the combination."

"Oh, great," Maureen said.

"What's the code? Hurry." I wiggled my fingers.

"You're making me nervous," he said. "Why are you so impatient?"

"You're nervous? How do you think I feel? No one can even see you. Plus, I'm in a locker room where I'm not supposed to be. It's like breaking and entering."

"Technically you didn't break in. You had the code," Maureen said.

"Exactly." Charlotte punctuated the sentence with a point of her finger.

"Okay, enough." I waved my hands. "Just give me the code."

Ramon ran his hand through his hair. "Okay, okay. Three."

I moved the dial and waited. There was a long pause. My heart sped up. The longer he took, the more likely I would be caught.

"Seven."

Whew. Now we were moving. I turned the dial again.

"Six."

I moved it around to the number. "How many more?"

"Five. That's the last one."

I hurried over to the number five. I sure hoped he had this right. If it didn't work, I was out of there. Time to abandon the mission. The lock clicked, and I pulled on the door.

"It worked," I said with relief.

"See, when you don't pressure me, I can figure things out," Ramon said.

"Yeah, Cookie. You need to calm down," Charlotte said.

I looked around the locker. "You have a lot of junk in here. You ever think of cleaning it out?" I asked.

"It is a pigsty," Charlotte said as she leaned against the lockers.

"I thought about it, but never got around to it." Ramon shrugged. "I suppose it doesn't matter now, does it?"

"Well, other than someone else will have to do it for you now," I said.

I stuck my hand in, afraid of what I might find. He had dirty clothing, magazines, books, shoes, and a mountain of equipment. I had no idea what all the equipment was used for.

"I don't even know what I'm looking for. There's nothing important in here."

"Take a look at that duffel bag." Charlotte pointed.

"Do I have to?" I asked.

"Come on, Cookie," Maureen said. "Suck it up, buttercup."

Easy for them to say; they were invisible. I took in a deep breath and grabbed the duffel bag. I set it on the ground and unzipped it.

"You act as if you're going to find a bomb," Charlotte said.

"I assure you there are no bombs in there," Ramon said.

"Good to know," I said as I shoved my hand inside and pulled out a couple of pieces of clothing.

"Take everything out," Charlotte instructed.

I pulled out more clothes. "More of the same." That was when I saw the envelope. "Wait. Here's something."

I pulled it out and read the address on the front. "It's a letter from Lewis."

"Who's Lewis?" Maureen asked.

"You remember, he owns the horse that Ramon was going to ride in the Derby."

"Oh yes," Maureen said with a chuckle.

"What does it say?" Charlotte asked, motioning for me to hurry and read the letter.

"I'm reading. Hold on." I scanned the letter.

"Well?" Charlotte asked.

"Lewis explains to Ramon that he can't have more money. And he doesn't appreciate Ramon's behavior," I said, casting a glance at Ramon. "What is this about? Were you asking for more money?"

Ramon grabbed at the letter, but his hand went right through it.

Charlotte laughed. "Newbie. You will have to practice a lot before you can move anything. Things have changed now that you're a ghost."

He scowled, not the least bit amused.

I moved the letter away. "Why are you trying to get this? I've already read it now. So? What's this all about?"

Ramon paced across the room. "Okay, yes, I asked for more money. What's the big deal?"

"The big deal is it seems as if you were threatening him. Was that why he referenced your behavior?" I asked.

"That's not very nice, Ramon," Charlotte said with a click of her tongue.

"Bad. Very bad." Maureen waved her finger.

"Okay, let's give Ramon a chance to explain."

Though I wasn't sure there was any explanation for this. The letter was pretty clear. He wanted more money; otherwise, he would start doing things that the owner wouldn't like.

I read more of the letter. "He told him he would lose the race on purpose."

Charlotte gasped. "That's just downright rotten. Lower than a snake's belly."

A noise echoed through the room.

"Someone's coming," Charlotte whispered.

I had to get out of there. I stuffed the belongings back into the locker and eased it shut. If someone saw me, they'd think I was stealing something. Footsteps sounded from the other side of the lockers. The person was walking down the next aisle. Someone whistled. I hoped they had no idea I was there. Pressing my back against the lockers, I inched along, trying not to make a sound. I couldn't breathe. The noise from the locker door being closed made me jump. I froze on the spot. What would I do next?

"I'll see what the person is doing," Charlotte said.

Maureen followed Charlotte around the corner.

"Whoa," Charlotte called out.

"My eyes, my eyes," Maureen screeched.

"He doesn't have a stitch on," Charlotte said as she ran back over to me.

Maureen was hot on her trail. I had to make a run for it. There was no way I wanted to be stuck in the locker room with a naked man. The distance to the door seemed to stretch on forever. Relief washed over me when I made it to the door.

"What are you doing in here?" the man asked.

He was standing there with nothing more than a towel wrapped around his waist.

I yanked the door open and ran out without saying a word. "I hope I never see that guy again."

I'd managed to get into Ramon's locker. Now I had even more unanswered questions. The letter from Lewis to Ramon gave Lewis a motive for murder. Lewis had plainly told Ramon that he couldn't have more money. Ramon admitted he was trying to get more money from Lewis. What had Ramon been thinking?

Chapter 10

Cookie's Savvy Tips for Vintage Shopping

Nothing haunts you like the things you didn't buy.
If you like something, buy it
because it will probably be gone
if you return to purchase it.

Just as I got back to the bed-and-breakfast, my phone rang.

"Oh, it's Heather," I said excitedly.

I was having fun in Kentucky, but I missed Heather and being back home. Wind Song weaved around my legs as I walked across the room.

"How is it mingling with the celebrities?" Heather asked.

I knew she didn't want to mention the murder. I hadn't told her yet that Ramon was attached to me.

"No mingling for me," I said as I sat on the bed.

"Well, maybe soon. Listen, there's a reason I called other than that I miss you."

"What's that?" I asked.

"Your mother and I have been thinking about Maureen's killer."

"Really? What about it?"

"There's something you need to do. You need to get a Ouija board for Wind Song."

Wind Song was sleeping on the chair by the window.

"Why do I need to do that?"

"Well, you don't have one, and I'm sure she has a lot to say"

Heather was probably right.

I sighed. "Where would I find something like that?"

"There are several occult shops nearby. I took the liberty of looking them up for you. I even mapped them out to find the one closest to the bed-and-breakfast where you're staying." Heather's words were rushed. She always talked fast when she was excited.

"Sounds like you have this all planned out," I said.

"Write this address down," she said. "You can put it in your phone to get the directions."

I'd rather have Heather here with me to find this place. After writing down the address, I clicked off of the call with Heather. I wondered what the bed-and-breakfast owner would think if I brought back a Ouija board. Yeah, that was something I wouldn't tell her. She'd kick me out for sure for something like that.

After feeding Wind Song, I tiptoed down the stairs and out the front door. I got into the Buick with the ghosts and headed in the direction of the occult shop. At least I hoped that was where I was headed. Fingers crossed that Heather had looked up the right place. The traffic was making me nervous as people whizzed from lane to lane and cut each other off.

"We're looking for Third Street," I said. "I think it's close to Churchill Downs."

"There it is." Charlotte pointed to the exit sign.

I whizzed the car over and got off the highway.

"I thought you said you were from a small town. You're driving as if you were in New York City," Ramon said from the backseat.

"I lived in Atlanta for a while." I merged into the other lane.

"Maybe we should have called this place to make sure they have the boards," Maureen said.

"That's probably an item they keep in stock," Ramon said. "I know where you're going now. I've been to this place before."

"You have?" I asked.

"Yes, with a friend."

"Your friend does magic?"

"I guess you could say that," he said.

Ramon was being cryptic. It sounded like he didn't want to tell me more.

I spotted the sign for the shop. It was black with white letters that read MOON AND EARTH. Smaller letters underneath the phrase spelled out MAGIC HAPPENS next to a drawing of a moon and clouds. Now I just needed to find a place to park.

"There's a spot." Charlotte pointed to a space between a van and a truck.

"Do you actually think I can squeeze this car into that tiny space?" I asked as I passed up the spot.

"Well, you won't know until you try," Charlotte said.

"Oh, I know already. I've been driving this big beauty for a while now, and I know there is no way."

"If you say so." Charlotte studied her finger-nails.

She did that a lot when I didn't do as she said.

"Look, here's a parking lot. I can park here." I whipped into a small parking lot at the side of a building.

I pulled the car into the first available space, got out, and headed for the sidewalk. A slight breeze caressed my skin. Not a single cloud appeared in the brilliant blue sky. The bell on the door announced us as the ghosts and I stepped into the shop. It was so dark in the space that I could barely see.

The smell of incense lingered in the air. It reminded me of Heather's shop back home, which made me homesick. I had to get hold of myself. I would only be gone for a few days. This shop had a lot more novelty items and fewer spices and herbs than Heather's. I liked her place much better, but I was a little biased.

"There's that smell again," Charlotte said, waving her hand in front of her nose.

"You can't smell anything," I whispered. "You're just being dramatic."

"As usual," Maureen added.

"Whose side are you on?" Charlotte frowned at Maureen.

"Were you talking to me?" a male voice asked from over my shoulder.

I jumped and spun around, clutching my chest. I had no idea anyone was behind me. How would I explain this one away? The young man wore a black T-shirt and jeans. His blond hair reached to just above his shoulders. It looked as if he'd just gotten out of bed.

"Do you work here?" I asked, trying to avoid answering his question.

Maybe he would forget that he'd caught me talking to myself.

"Yes, I work here. May I help you find something?"

"I'm looking for a Ouija board."

He stared at me. "Are you sure you want one of those things? They can be dangerous."

"He's quite a salesman." Charlotte chuckled.

"I take the necessary precautions," I said.

He studied my face. "Follow me."

I walked behind him across the room to the far wall. A small stack of the boards were piled at the bottom of a bookshelf. Charlotte pushed a book from the shelf. It landed with a thud on the hardwood floor. The guy jumped back and looked at me with wide eyes.

"You've been using the Ouija board already. Did you bring a ghost here with you?" he asked.

"Oh, he's good." Charlotte walked in a circle around the guy.

He followed her trail as if he saw her. "I feel the cold air around me."

I didn't have time to explain everything to him. "I've used the board before, but I don't think there's a ghost here."

"There most definitely is, but you probably just don't sense it like I do. You should try to get them to move on to the light."

Fat chance of that happening.

Charlotte and Maureen chuckled.

"He's so cute and naïve," Charlotte said.

"You should ask if he remembers seeing Ramon in here," Maureen said.

"He wouldn't remember me. There are a lot of people coming in and out of this shop."

"Yes, but maybe he knows you since you're a jockey," Charlotte said.

Charlotte had a point.

After the guy handed me the Ouija board, I asked, "I think someone I know came in here."

"Oh really?" he asked as he moved over to the counter.

"He's a jockey at Churchill Downs."

"Not just Churchill Downs," Ramon said.

That was neither here nor there.

"He had dark hair and mesmerizing blue eyes."

"Thanks," Ramon said.

He pointed. "Hey, I remember him. He was in

here with a woman. She had a spooky vibe." The guy shivered.

"What do you mean?" I asked.

"She gave me the chills the second she walked into this place. When she looked at me, I actually shook a little."

I had my suspicions that the person he described was Mandy. Ramon was leaving out a lot of information. He claimed he hadn't had an affair with Mandy, but it seemed as if they spent a lot of time together. I would press him for more details.

"Thanks for the information," I said.

"No problem." He rang up the board. "That'll be thirty-four ninety-five."

"Wow, that's an expensive toy," Charlotte said.

It was pricey, but Charlotte had spent that much for a bottle of nail polish when she'd been alive.

I gathered the board under my arm. "Thanks again."

"Just be careful," the guy warned again.

Once out on the sidewalk, I said, "I can't take you two anywhere."

Charlotte looked at me with an innocent stare. "What? We were just having fun."

"I don't think it was fun for that guy. He was scared."

"Did you see his face? It looked as if he was ready to run for his life," Maureen said with a chuckle.

Chapter 11

Grandma Pearl's Pearls of Wisdom

*Just because a chicken has wings
doesn't mean it can fly.*

I made it back to my car and climbed behind the
wheel, placing the Ouija board on the seat beside
me. I couldn't believe I had actually bought one.
When Heather first brought one to my shop for
Wind Song to use, I wouldn't even let her keep it
there. I was concerned it would bring in bad
spirits. So far that hadn't happened.

"I just think it is so nice of you to do this for
us," Maureen said.

"Thank you. You're welcome, Maureen."

"See, Cookie really loves a good mystery,"
Charlotte said.

"I really don't think I should use the board at the

bed-and-breakfast," I said as I made the next left turn. "What if I accidentally brought in evil spirits?"

"Where will you use it if not at the bed-and-breakfast?" Maureen asked.

"I think I saw a park close by. We could stop and pick up Wind Song and go over there."

"Sounds like a good place to me," Charlotte said. "Though I doubt you will bring in any bad spirits. It hasn't happened yet."

"No, but it is a nice thing to do, right? Just in case." I steered the car around a turn. "Plus, what if now was the time that a bad spirit found its way through? I would never forgive myself for that."

For the rest of the drive, we were lost in thought listening to The Platters sing "The Magic Touch." Hannah would definitely know I was up to something when I returned to pick up the cat. After parking the car out front, I slipped in the front door. I paused. All was quiet. I couldn't believe that Hannah wasn't waiting at the door for me. I eased up the stairs, trying not to make them squeak. Of course, the treads made a sound with almost each step.

"She must be asleep," Charlotte said.

The hinges groaned as I eased my door open. Wind Song was on the chair by the window. She wagged her tail as soon as she saw me.

"Grandma Pearl, we're going for a ride," I whispered.

I picked her up and carried her out into the hallway. Now that I knew she wouldn't run away, I didn't have to bother with the carrier, although sometimes I had to use it just so people wouldn't be suspicious.

After placing Wind Song in the car, we hurried back to the park. My headlights flashed across the entrance sign as I turned in. Tall pine trees surrounded us like soldiers guarding the park.

"This place is scary," Charlotte said.

"It looks spooky during the day too," Ramon said. "I've heard ghost stories about this place."

Maureen waved her hands. "Oh, I don't even want to hear the stories. I think I'll stay in the car."

It was funny that the ghosts were scared of other ghosts. Pulling over into a small parking area, I parked the car close to a picnic bench and picked up Wind Song. With my other hand, I grabbed the Ouija board.

"Come on, guys. Don't make me go out there alone," I said.

The ghosts reluctantly got out of the car and followed me over to the picnic table. The night was silent except for an owl hooting in the distance. First, I placed the board down. Next was Wind Song.

"Okay, Grandma. Heather said you'd be able to tell us something about Maureen's killer."

Wind Song meowed and placed her paw on the planchette.

"Wow, you weren't kidding. The cat really can use the board," Ramon said as he watched with wide eyes.

Wind Song moved the planchette around to different letters. I had to keep up so I'd know what she was spelling. Heather usually liked to write down the letters when she was around. Wind Song stopped.

"What did she say?" Charlotte asked.

Maureen looked as if she was afraid to find out.

"She said that someone who claimed to love Maureen was responsible for Maureen's death."

We all looked at Maureen. She stood completely still, with a shocked look on her face.

"The cat said all that?" Ramon asked.

"Well, I'm completing the message for her," I said.

"Do you know who that would be?" Charlotte asked Maureen.

Maureen shook her head.

"A lot of murders are perpetrated by people who claim to love you." I stroked Wind Song's back.

"That doesn't tell us much," Charlotte said.

"I'm sure Grandma Pearl is working on it."

I wasn't sure how Grandma Pearl got her information. Maybe she had some special informant on the other side.

"Okay, it's creepy out here. Can we leave now?" Ramon peered around as if he'd heard something.

I picked up Wind Song and the board. "Sure, let's go."

As I walked across the grassy area toward the car, a rustling noise caught my attention. Wind Song hissed and wiggled in my arms.

"What was that?" I whispered.

"I don't know, but don't stop now. Get in the car." Charlotte urged.

Maureen and Ramon had already rushed back to the Buick. We got back into the car, and I locked the doors. I shoved the car into reverse and sped toward the park's entrance. Once back on the lonely stretch of road, I pointed the car toward the bed-and-breakfast. I didn't think it was possible, but the road seemed even spookier now. Headlights appeared behind me.

"Where did that car come from?" I asked, glancing in the rearview mirror.

"I don't know, but they're following too close." Charlotte turned around in her seat.

Luckily, I'd made it to the turnoff for the bed-and-breakfast. The car sped past. I couldn't make out what kind it was, only that it was a dark color. Maybe that was why I hadn't seen it until it was directly behind me. I'd probably passed it as I drove down that dark road.

The bed-and-breakfast was just as I'd left it. Not a single light shone from the windows. The sun had set hours ago, and I knew Hannah would be upset that I'd stayed out so late. With any luck, she'd be asleep.

"Maybe I should leave the Ouija board in the car, just in case," I said as I shut off the engine.

"That's probably a good idea," Charlotte said as she zipped out of the car.

Wind Song came over to me, and I picked her up. The ghosts were waiting on the porch for me.

Soft murmurs of the night carried across the air as I hurried toward the front door.

Before I eased the door open, I tiptoed over to the window. The house was quiet, but a small light shone from the living room.

I motioned. "Look. I think I'm in trouble."

"Oh, this lady is ridiculous. She needs a hobby," Charlotte said.

I opened the door and inched across the room.

"Cookie, is that you?" Hannah called out.

I wouldn't lie; her monitoring my every move was slightly annoying.

"It's barely ten o'clock. I really don't think it should be lights out yet," I said as I stomped into the room.

"Oh, she's going to kick you out of here now," Charlotte followed me.

When I spotted Dylan Valentine, I stopped in my tracks.

Chapter 12

Cookie's Savvy Tips for Vintage Shopping

*Examine vintage pieces in the light.
You'll want to notice if there are
holes or other flaws.*

Dylan rushed over to me and wrapped his arms around me. His thick, dark hair was styled in a short cut and stood up just a little in the front. Dylan's fit physique was evident underneath his well-fitting clothing. His brilliant blue eyes sent a jolt through me every time he looked my way. Dylan looked handsome in his tan slacks and black button-down, short-sleeved shirt. He was a total dreamboat. His eyes lit up when he smiled.

"What are you doing here?" I asked. "Is everything okay with my mother and Heather?"

A sudden panic rushed through me.

"They're fine. I just got the idea that I should

come see you. I figured why not? I had some time off saved up anyway." He leaned down and pressed his lips against mine.

"I'm glad you came."

"Mr. Valentine was telling me that he's an officer back in Georgia."

"I think she's been charmed by the detective as well." Charlotte winked.

Dylan had a way of doing that to everyone. His charisma and smile were intoxicating.

"Are you staying here too?" I asked.

He gestured toward Hannah. "She doesn't have any other rooms available, so I booked one at the Holiday Inn down the road."

It wasn't so down the road. The nearest Holiday Inn had to be a ten-minute drive.

"So much for Dylan charming her." Charlotte huffed.

I knew Hannah wasn't telling the truth. She had extra rooms, but it was her place and her decision whether to rent them or not.

"I'll leave you two alone for just a bit. Don't be too long. And no hanky-panky." Hannah warned with a wave of her finger.

She disappeared into the kitchen. Dylan quirked an eyebrow.

"She makes a good breakfast," I said. "Other than that, her innkeeper skills are lacking."

"So I noticed. Anyway, I'm so happy to see you." Dylan touched my arm.

I still couldn't believe he'd driven all this way to see me.

"He just couldn't bear the thought of being without you for another minute." Charlotte pretended to swoon.

"Isn't it sweet?" Maureen added.

This was one time I agreed with Maureen and Charlotte. Dylan was sweet. He leaned down and kissed my lips again.

"Oh, things just took a romantic turn," Charlotte said.

"Maybe we should leave the lovebirds alone," Ramon said.

Charlotte and Maureen ignored him.

"Ladies?" Ramon said in a sterner voice.

The ghosts gave in and disappeared around the corner. They wouldn't go far.

"I guess I should be going so that Hannah doesn't get upset."

I sighed. "Yeah. I guess so."

"Walk me to my car?" Dylan asked with a smile.

"Sure."

I wondered if I needed to ask Hannah's permission for that too. She returned into the room and looked at her watch.

"I'll be right back," I called over my shoulder.

"Nice meeting you, Hannah." Dylan tossed his hand up in a wave.

"Likewise," Hannah said.

Dylan and I stepped out into the lovely night air. It didn't seem nearly as spooky with Dylan by my side. Crickets chirped from the nearby trees, and the stars dazzled in the dark sky. Suddenly romance hung in the air.

Dylan leaned against my car and pulled me close. His spicy scent was wrapping me in a hug as well.

"I didn't see your car when I pulled up." I looked around.

"I wanted to surprise you, so I parked around the side."

"Well, it worked. I was surprised." I looked him in the eyes. "You really came because you were worried about the murder, isn't that right?"

He studied my face. "That was part of it, yes. I just wanted to make sure you were okay."

He should know by now that I was pretty good at taking care of myself. Although sometimes I needed a little help from my friends. Who doesn't on occasion?

"I've been looking into who may have done this to the jockey." I rubbed my arms to fight off the slight chill of the spring night.

He hugged me again to keep me warm. "Why would you do that? It's dangerous."

Unfortunately, I couldn't tell him it was because the ghost of the murder victim was following me around. Although I knew that wasn't the only reason I was doing it. Actually, there were a number of reasons. Number one was there was a murderer out there who needed to be behind bars. The porch light flickered, and I knew it was

Hannah's warning that it was time to come inside. It was like being in high school all over again.

Dylan brushed the hair from my forehead. "How about breakfast in the morning? There's a little place around the corner from where I'm staying."

"I can meet you there since I want to check out a couple of thrift shops tomorrow."

Dylan smiled. "How's eight?"

"Eight sounds great."

He kissed me good-bye and watched as I headed up the porch to the front door. It was sweet that he wanted to make sure I got back inside safely. I must admit that the bed-and-breakfast had a spooky vibe. Despite being a short drive to shops and restaurants, it felt isolated.

I'd just stepped in the door and Dylan had pulled away when the ghosts popped up in front of me.

I jumped. "Don't do that. You scared me."

"You'd think you'd be used to ghosts by now," Charlotte said.

"I'm used to ghosts. What I'm not used to is people popping up in front of me unannounced." I peered over into the living room. Where was Hannah?

"How did it go?" Charlotte asked with a smile.

"It's fine." I couldn't hold back a smile when I thought about Dylan.

"It's a good thing he's here. Now maybe he can

talk to the police." Charlotte walked over to the living room door and peered in too.

"That's a good idea," Ramon said.

I peeked around to see if the owner was standing nearby. Maybe she'd gone to bed.

"I plan to go to the police tomorrow and ask questions."

Charlotte snorted. "They're not going to tell you anything."

"Thanks for the vote of confidence," I whispered.

Charlotte held her hands up. "Just stating the truth."

"It's true. They probably won't talk to you," Ramon said.

"Better to let Dylan do it," Maureen added.

I narrowed my eyes. "I'll show you all. I will get something out of them. Besides, Dylan hasn't even said he would talk to the police."

"He would if you asked him," Charlotte said.

"I won't need to ask him because I will ask the police myself."

Out of the corner of my eye, I spotted Hannah. She was staring at me. "Who are you talking to?"

"Oh, she's really going to kick you out now," Maureen said.

I should have sneaked back to my room while I had the chance. What would I say?

I pulled the phone from my pocket. "Just making a phone call."

"Oh, nice try," Charlotte said.

"Well, I guess I'll go to bed now. Good night." I tossed my hand up in a wave.

She didn't take her eyes off me as I headed up the stairs. Hannah didn't have to say a word for me to know what was on her mind. She thought I'd lost my marbles.

Chapter 13

Grandma Pearl's Pearls of Wisdom

*Beauty is only skin deep,
but ugly goes clean to the bone.*

The next morning, I jumped out of bed, ready to start the day.

"Look how fast she moves when she knows she's meeting Dylan." Charlotte stood by the door, looking at her fingernails.

"I heard that," I said as I finished brushing my teeth.

I put down the brush and headed for the closet.

"To be honest, I'd move that quickly too if I had a handsome man like that waiting on me," Maureen said as she sat in the chair by the window.

"What to wear?" I said as I looked at the dresses I'd brought.

"Wear the striped one," Charlotte said.

I decided on a 1950s cotton dress with blue

roses that cascaded down the fabric. It had a full skirt and a sleeveless bodice. A blue-ribbon belt was tied around the waist. I paired the dress with my red sandals with three-inch heels. A tiny strap was fastened with a gold buckle around the ankle.

"You look pretty," Ramon said.

"Thank you, Ramon," I said as I buckled the strap on my sandal.

Before I met Dylan for breakfast, I decided to visit the police station. The ghosts thought I wouldn't be able to get any information from the detectives. I wanted to prove them wrong. How I would achieve that, I didn't know. I'd grabbed some coffee and slipped away from the house before Hannah realized I was gone. I didn't have time for small talk this morning.

I pulled up to the police station. Thank goodness, I hadn't gotten lost trying to find the place. It was tucked away in a building that houses other businesses. It looked more like a warehouse, but it was just a small substation for the area. The big precinct was downtown.

"This isn't the restaurant." Charlotte frowned. "What are you up to?"

"I'm going to talk with the detective first."

Charlotte scoffed. "Good luck, Cookie. I just think that you should ask Dylan to do that. There's nothing wrong with asking for a little help."

"No, there's nothing wrong with it, but I have to try things for myself first." I shut off the engine.

Maureen and Ramon had already gotten out of the car. Apparently, they were eager.

I got out from behind the wheel and closed the door. Once I was inside the station, the young officer behind the desk asked if he could help me. This place was a lot busier than the station in Sugar Creek.

"I would like to speak with Detective Anderson, please."

"What is your name?"

"Cookie Chanel. I found the jockey at the museum event at Churchill Downs."

The officer looked me up and down as he picked up the phone. He turned his back away from me so that I couldn't hear what he said. When he hung up, he said, "Detective Anderson will be with you soon."

Stepping away from the counter, I gave the ghosts a smirk.

"No need to get cocky, Cookie," Charlotte said.

Maureen and Ramon laughed.

"Go ahead and make fun," I said. "I'll get the last laugh."

A couple of seconds later, the detective called out to me. He'd probably overheard me talking to the ghosts. His dark hair had just a sprinkling of gray. His white button-down shirt was rolled up at the sleeves and tucked into his tan slacks. His blue tie was loose, as if he wanted to take the thing off.

"May I help you?" he asked.

"Detective, I'm the one who discovered Ramon."

"Yes, I remember."

"You're unforgettable, Cookie," Charlotte said. "Not necessarily in a good way though."

"What can I do for you?" He studied my face.

"Do you have any leads in the case?"

"You can't just come out and ask him that." Charlotte tossed her hands up.

Okay, maybe I didn't have the best plan, but at least my question was out there now. I'd asked, and there was no taking it back, no pretending I was here for another reason.

"I can't discuss the case. Sorry," he said. "Do you have any information for us?"

He eyed me suspiciously, as if I'd been withholding details. How would I tell the detective about the letter I'd found and overhearing the conversation? I liked Lewis and Elise, but I couldn't hide the fact that one of them could possibly be the killer.

"Um, actually I overheard Elise on the phone," I said.

"I thought you were getting information, not giving," Maureen said.

The detective shoved his hands into his pockets. "Tell me more."

"She just basically said she didn't mind if Ramon was dead because now she could find a better jockey."

"That's doubtful," Ramon said.

"Basically?" The detective quirked a bushy eyebrow. "Can you tell me word for word what was said?"

"I don't think I remember exactly."

"I can tell you," Ramon said. "I'll never forget her hurtful words."

Okay, now I had to pretend as if I'd remembered.

"Well, maybe I can remember," I said.

Ramon repeated the conversation to refresh my memory.

"Elise said she wasn't sorry that he wasn't riding the horse. Because he wouldn't do as he was told."

"We'll look into it," the detective said. "Let me know if you think of anything else."

"That means he wants you to get lost," Maureen said.

Yeah, I got the hint.

"Thanks. I will," I said.

The ghosts and I walked out into the parking lot. I suppose they had proved me wrong. I'd gotten zero information.

"Will he look into it? He doesn't seem interested in finding my killer," Ramon said.

"I'm sure he wants to find the killer. It just takes time," I said as I opened the car door.

I slipped behind the wheel and cranked the engine.

"You need to have a plan, Cookie. Winging it doesn't work," Charlotte said from the passenger seat."

"You don't need the cops anyway," Maureen said from the backseat.

When I arrived at the restaurant, I pulled into the spot right next to Dylan's car.

"He must be waiting for you inside," Charlotte said.

"Are you all going to talk in my ear the whole time I'm in there?" I asked. "You know I can't answer."

"Aren't you testy this morning," Charlotte said.

"She must be hungry," Maureen said.

"I think it's time that you told Dylan about us," Charlotte said.

"He doesn't know?" Ramon asked.

"It's not good to keep secrets," Maureen said. "That's no way to start a relationship. How would you like it if he was keeping secrets from you?"

I looked in the rearview mirror at her. "He'll think I'm bonkers if I tell him."

"You might be surprised by how understanding he is," Ramon said.

I got out of the car and closed the door.

"What kind of place is this anyway?" Charlotte peered around.

The diner was a bit eccentric, but it looked fun. It was a retro-style building and had colorful statues of animals all around the parking lot. A large horse with polka dots stood in front of the door. I stepped inside and saw that the front lobby was a gift shop full of kitschy novelty items. Colors of turquoise and pink decorated the place. Booths and tables filled the dining room.

"This looks like your style, right out of the fifties," Charlotte said.

The petite hostess looked at me and said, "You must be Cookie."

"Yes," I said.

"Follow me," she said with a wave of her hand.

Charlotte and Maureen laughed.

"Dylan must have described you," Charlotte said.

I spotted Dylan as soon as we reached the dining area. He smiled broadly when our eyes met.

"Here you are. The waitress will be with you soon." She placed a menu down on the table in front of me.

I slipped into the booth across from Dylan. The smell of syrup and coffee lingered in the air.

"How do you like the place?" I asked.

"It's unusual, but I love it so far." He took a sip of coffee.

"Unusual like Cookie," Charlotte said.

The ghosts had slipped into the empty booth right behind us. Now they would eavesdrop on the entire conversation. Not to mention add commentary too.

I picked up the menu and scanned the options. "I think I'll have the blueberry pancakes."

Dylan smiled. "French toast for me."

After placing our orders, Dylan took a sip of his orange juice and looked at me. "I thought maybe you weren't coming this morning."

"You were only ten minutes late," Charlotte said, with her arms resting on the back of my seat.

She was turned all the way around in the

booth with her knees on the seat where her bottom should be.

"Tell him where you were and ask him to help," Ramon said.

"Good idea. That will give you more time to work on finding my killer," Maureen said.

So much chatter. How was I supposed to concentrate on Dylan?

A couple of minutes later, our food arrived. Blueberries were piled on top of the fluffy pancakes, and juice ran down the sides of the stack. Dylan's French toast had a dollop of whipped topping in the center.

"That looks delicious," Maureen said.

She was leaning over the back of my seat like a toddler now too.

"Dylan's looks good too," Charlotte said from the other side. "Oh, the sweet syrup and the melt-in-your-mouth butter."

The ghosts were getting carried away with the food. I took a few bites. While I chewed, I contemplated telling Dylan where I'd been. I traced tracks in the syrup with my fork.

"There was somewhere I went this morning before I came here," I said.

He paused with his fork in the air. "Really? Where's that?"

He finished his bite.

"I went by the police station and spoke with a detective." I studied his face for a reaction.

"He's awfully quiet," Charlotte said.

"You just now went . . . this morning?" he asked.

"Well, I didn't see that coming," Charlotte said.

"Honestly, I thought you would have gone a long time ago. What did the detective say?" he asked.

"He told me they really couldn't say much. I told him that I had overheard Elise on the phone. She was glad that Ramon wasn't going to ride the horse in the Derby."

Dylan took a drink from his mug and placed it back on the table. "Well, that doesn't mean Elise killed him."

"No, it doesn't, but it doesn't rule her out either." I wiped my mouth with the napkin.

He grinned. "No, you're right about that."

Charlotte appeared at the side of the table now. "You have to tell him about finding the letter."

I wanted to tell him, but I would have to admit that I had been snooping around. I suppose it wouldn't surprise him to hear that I'd done that. And he'd been understanding about my visit to the police station. But still . . .

I traced the rim of my glass with my finger, avoiding eye contact. "I was just thinking that maybe you could talk with the police."

"Cookie, this isn't my case. I don't work in Kentucky."

I looked up at him. "I think it's important that we find the killer. What if I'm working with the potential killer? Wouldn't you want to know?"

"Good job, Cookie," Maureen said.

"That will really get him," Charlotte said.

Dylan stared. "I guess I could talk to them. There's no guarantee that they'll tell me anything."

"I guess we'll have to search for clues ourselves."

"We?" he asked.

"I think we make a good team."

He smiled. "You're right about that. I think we make a good team too."

Every time Dylan said something like that, my stomach flipped and my body tingled. He had just the right amount of charm. Dylan was genuine.

We finished our breakfast, and Dylan paid the bill as I checked out the gifts at the front of the store. I definitely had to take my parents a souvenir. For my father, I bought a Kentucky shot glass, and my mother would receive a mug with cherries on it for her collection.

Dylan and I walked outside to our cars. A springtime breeze ruffled the leaves on a nearby magnolia tree. Golden beams of sunlight covered the area. Purple and yellow pansies cheerfully dotted the landscaping.

He opened the car door for me. "I'll see you later?"

"I want to check out some of the thrift stores, but there's an event tonight. I'd love it if you could come with me."

"Tell me what time to pick you up, and I'll be there."

I smiled. "How about seven?"

He leaned down and kissed me. "See you later."

I slipped into my car, and Dylan closed the door for me. I watched as he walked over to his car.

"I can't believe he agreed to talk with the police," Ramon said.

"You should believe it, Ramon. Dylan is in love." Charlotte winked.

Chapter 14

Check for missing buttons or faulty zippers.
Also look for stitching that may need repair.

Before I left the restaurant parking lot, my cell phone rang.

"Dylan misses you already," Charlotte said.

"Sorry, Charlotte, but this call is from Danielle." Charlotte frowned. "Too bad."

"Cookie, where are you?" Danielle asked when I answered.

Oh no, had I forgotten an appointment? "I had breakfast, and I'm checking out some of the thrift stores."

"Oh, you have to take me with you. Maybe we'll find a bargain."

She certainly was frugal for someone who has millions. Sometimes thrift shopping wasn't about the money though. It was more about the thrill of the hunt. I was just happy that I hadn't forgotten about something important. Once Dylan arrived, I had become a little distracted.

"Can you pick me up?" she asked.

"Sure. Are you at the hotel?" I asked.

"No, I'm at the backside."

"The backside?" I repeated.

"Of Churchill Downs. At the barn."

"Oh, good. I want to go back there," Ramon said.

"I'll be there soon." I headed toward Churchill Downs.

Traffic was heavy, so it would take at least thirty minutes to travel across town. I wished I could have found a closer place to stay. I was lucky I'd found the bed-and-breakfast, though I was beginning to see why she had vacancies.

Twenty-nine minutes later, I pulled up to the guard shack, and the man on duty waved me through this time. I suppose he remembered the car, though I didn't think it would be so easy to get back where all the horses were kept. I parked and headed over to the barn. The smell of manure and hay filled my nostrils. As I neared, the sound of raised voices carried across the spring air. One was Danielle's, and I soon realized the other was Mandy's. They were arguing.

"I know you took my stuff, so why don't you just admit it?" Danielle said.

"I can't believe you are accusing me of that," Mandy said.

"This place is like a soap opera," Maureen said.

Maybe I should have made my presence known, but I wanted to hear what this was all about.

"I saw you by the car," Danielle said.

"You must be mistaken," Mandy said.

"I think I know when I see something," Danielle said.

"I don't have to deal with this. I will talk to Lewis about this," Mandy said.

"Go right ahead. I don't know what good you think that will do," Danielle said.

"I'm going around the corner so I can see if they start throwing punches," Charlotte said.

"I'm coming with you." Maureen followed Charlotte.

Ramon stayed with me. "I don't want to deal with any more drama. I had enough of that when I was alive."

The arguing stopped. I hoped one of them didn't come around the corner and catch me eavesdropping. I stepped forward so that it would look as if I was just walking around the barn and that I hadn't heard a word of what they'd said. I bumped right into Mandy. She stopped and glared at me.

A fake smile spread across her face. "I'm sorry. I didn't know someone would walk around the barn like that."

"Wait just a cotton-pickin' minute. What is that supposed to mean?" Charlotte placed her hands on her hips.

Charlotte had a quick temper.

"I don't like the way she looked at you." Maureen walked a circle around Mandy.

"Ask her about the fight," Charlotte urged.

"Well, I'll see you," Mandy said as she stepped around me.

"Ask now, or you may not get a chance again," Maureen said.

I was nervous to ask—Mandy had an intimidating demeanor—but decided to do it anyway.

"Mandy, I couldn't help but overhear you arguing with Danielle as I came around the barn."

Now was the time she'd tell me to mind my own business.

She eyed me up and down.

"She is kind of scary, isn't she?" Charlotte said.

"She's not scary—"

"You just have to . . . get to know her." Charlotte finished Ramon's sentence for him.

Mandy crossed her arms in front of her chest. "Danielle is volatile. She's impossible to deal with. She had the nerve to accuse me of stealing from her. I would never do something like that." Mandy peered at me with a doe-eyed look.

"Tell her that flirty look doesn't work on you. Maybe it worked on Ramon," Charlotte said.

"She really upset me." Mandy stared at me as if she was waiting for me to say something.

What was I going to say? I liked Danielle. I didn't know the facts, so I certainly wasn't going to take sides.

"Well, I hope you all work things out," I said.

Mandy studied my face for a second longer. I noticed her jaw tighten. She was obviously upset that I hadn't immediately taken her side. Her stare was focused on me like a laser.

"To be honest, I think Danielle killed Ramon."

"Wow, that's a big accusation," I said.

She shrugged. "I'm just saying what I feel. I'd be careful around her if I were you."

I didn't know what to think of her warning.

"I'll take that into consideration."

"Nice talking to you," she said with another one of her fake smiles.

"You too," I said.

Mandy turned and strolled away. If she was concerned about Danielle, she didn't show it. She didn't mind fighting with her.

"What do you think of what she said?" Charlotte asked.

"I don't know what to think," I whispered.

We looked at Ramon. He had been quiet throughout the entire conversation.

"You know Mandy the best. What do you think?" I asked.

He shrugged. "You—"

"Just have to . . . get to know her," Charlotte, Maureen, and I finished his sentence.

"I need to talk with Danielle to get her side of the story." I eased around the side of the barn.

The horses made noise, announcing my presence. Danielle was standing by the office door. The scowl on her face let me know that she still wasn't happy. She forced a smile when she saw me.

"Is everything okay?" I asked.

"I just ran into Mandy." Danielle rolled her eyes. "I'm thinking about calling the police."

"What happened?" I asked, though I'd already gotten the story from Mandy. Well, her side at least.

"She took things from my car. There was my wallet, and I don't know what else she took."

"Why do you think she did that?" I asked.

"For one thing, she doesn't know how to manage her money."

Something pulled on my shirt. I spun around to find a horse trying to bite at my sleeve.

Danielle laughed. "He wants your attention."

I rubbed the horse.

"We should go," Danielle said. "I'll grab my stuff."

I knew she was still angry, but at least the horse had calmed her down.

After Danielle had her bag, we headed around the barn and toward my car.

"Maybe shopping will take my mind off everything," Danielle said.

"It always made me feel better," Charlotte said.

My car would be crowded with all the ghosts and Danielle. I hoped Charlotte wouldn't try to argue over who got the passenger seat this time. I'd have a hard time explaining that to Danielle.

As we walked across the area toward my car, I felt as if someone was watching us. When I looked over, I noticed Mandy. She was staring. I didn't point it out to Danielle. She was feeling a little better, and I didn't want to get her upset again.

Mandy realized that I had spotted her, but she didn't smile back when I smiled at her.

"She gives me the creeps," Charlotte whispered.

"Me too," I said.

"What was that?" Danielle asked.

"Oh . . . I said, I can't wait to shop."

She quirked an eyebrow but said nothing else about my strange comment. We walked in silence until we reached the car. Thank goodness, Mandy wasn't still watching us. Charlotte was nice enough not to argue and got into the backseat with the other ghosts. As soon as I pulled out onto the road, a large black truck veered over into the lane in front of me. I blasted the horn and swerved to avoid a collision. The truck didn't slow down.

"It was as if they did that on purpose," Charlotte said.

"Are you okay?" I asked Danielle.

She pushed the hair out of her eyes. "Yes, I'm fine. That was a close one."

If I'd wrecked the car, I didn't know what I would have done. Danielle gave me directions on how to get to the shop. Traffic was even worse now. I missed the rush hour of Sugar Creek, which was nothing compared to this.

"Did Mandy say anything else to you?" Danielle asked.

There was no way I would admit that Mandy had accused Danielle of being the murderer. That was when it hit me. Could Danielle be the murderer? No, she was too nice. Although just because she was nice to me didn't mean she couldn't be mean to others.

"No, nothing at all." I smiled.

"Let me see if I can piece this together," Charlotte said from the backseat.

Danielle had no idea that a ghost was talking. What would she do if she'd known? My best guess was that she would probably freak out.

Charlotte continued. "Cookie overheard Danielle and Mandy arguing. Danielle accused Mandy of stealing from her."

"Right." Maureen leaned forward in the seat.

"Cookie bumped into Mandy, who admitted that she'd had arguments in the past with Danielle."

"Mandy said that Danielle is volatile," Maureen added.

"She accused Danielle of murdering Ramon. According to Mandy, Danielle argued with Ramon days before his murder. That's not something you can take lightly, Cookie," Charlotte said.

"Not to be taken lightly at all," Maureen said with a click of her tongue.

I'd keep all of that in mind.

We arrived at the shop, and I parked the car along the street. Second Time Around was located in a brick building that had several other stores. Lush green landscaping and a bubbling stone water fountain welcomed shoppers. People strolled down the sidewalk and in and out of the shops.

"I think I'll wait outside," Ramon said.

I wasn't surprised. He didn't seem interested in shopping. Danielle and I walked into the shop.

Faint music played in the background. It was crammed full of clothing. I wasn't sure where to even start. There was such a thing as too much. The cramped space almost made me dizzy. Racks, tables, and shelves were full of clothing, shoes, and accessories. I was on sensory overload. It was a bit too dim in the space as well.

"Is there anything I can help you with?" the woman asked from behind the counter.

"We're just looking," Danielle said.

"I feel like I can't breathe in here." Charlotte held her neck as if she was struggling for air.

Too bad I couldn't remind her right now that she didn't need air.

"We should look at the dresses first," Danielle said as she motioned for me to follow her.

Danielle and I picked out a handful of dresses and carried them to the changing rooms. I had selected a Calvin Klein sleeveless brown and white polka-dot dress with a full skirt and a fitted bodice. The design was from the late eighties. I also had a pair of untagged pale yellow cigarette pants from the fifties and a light pink cardigan sweater from the eighties that was styled to look like the fifties. Hey, vintage was vintage. The year never mattered, only that it looked good.

Danielle had a Thierry Mugler emerald-green silk dress from the eighties that I knew would accentuate her curves. The color would look amazing on her. I stepped into the room and pulled the curtain closed. When I turned around, Charlotte and Maureen were there with me. I motioned for them to get out.

"We can't see anything out there," Charlotte said.

I pointed again with a stern look, since I couldn't talk to them right now. Charlotte and Maureen stomped out of the room, and I tried on the dress.

"Cookie," Charlotte called from the other side of the dressing room wall. "Since Danielle is calmed down now, maybe you could tell her what Mandy said."

Danielle seemed to be having a good time. Why would I ruin it now by bringing up Mandy? Though I would like to hear what Danielle said about it.

"Danielle, how's it going?" I asked.

"I'm coming out," she said.

I stepped out of the dressing room. "Just as I thought. That color looks fantastic on you."

"That dress looks amazing on you," Danielle pointed out.

"Enough of the mutual admiration society. Tell her about Mandy," Charlotte said.

"Danielle," I said.

She looked at me in the reflection of the mirror as she admired her dress.

"There was something that Mandy said. I just didn't want to upset you."

"I knew it." Danielle spun around to face me. "What did she say?"

Maureen and Charlotte were staring.

I cleared my throat. "Well, she said she suspected you of murdering Ramon. She said you were volatile."

Danielle's face turned scarlet red, and she cursed under her breath.

"She's really mad," Charlotte said.

I knew she would be mad. That was why I hadn't wanted to tell her.

"Is that right?" Danielle placed her hands on her hips. "What do you think?"

My eyes widened. "I don't think you had anything to do with it."

"Do you think I'm volatile?" She quirked an eyebrow.

I sensed that I was supposed to say no, even if I didn't think that.

"No, of course not."

"You didn't sound very convincing," Charlotte said.

"I think you're making her madder," Maureen said.

They were the ones making this worse.

I waved my hand. "Get changed, and we can buy this stuff. Don't even worry about what Mandy said."

Danielle stared at me for a bit. With a furrowed brow and a frown, her look was not a happy one. She turned and walked back into the dressing room. I hurried back after her.

"Well, that went well, Cookie." Charlotte said. "By the way, that dress does nothing for you."

Just wait until I could talk to Charlotte and

Maureen. Danielle was already at the counter when I stepped out of the dressing rooms. I wondered how long she would be mad. This would be an awkward drive back. I knew I shouldn't have mentioned Mandy.

Danielle spoke again as we made it to the car. Thank goodness, she still wasn't mad at me. What if she was the killer and I was riding around with her? I had to push that thought out of my mind. I pulled out onto the road. As we drove along, I noticed a truck on the left. It was just sitting there.

"Doesn't that look like the truck that tried to cut us off the road?" Danielle asked.

"Actually, I think it is the truck. I suppose it's just a coincidence that it's here too," I said as I hurried through the light.

I peered in the rearview mirror to see if the truck had followed us. Luckily, it wasn't behind us.

"I'll keep an eye out for the truck," Charlotte said.

It looked as if she wouldn't have to because the truck remained parked. It was just a coincidence. Thank goodness, the rest of the trip was uneventful. I'd had enough excitement for the day. Danielle never mentioned Mandy again for the rest of the trip.

After dropping off Danielle at the backside, I hoped that she wouldn't have any more arguments with Mandy, especially now that I'd told her what Mandy had said. The more I thought about it, the more I realized I should have kept that part to myself. Danielle waved at the car as I pulled away. I'd see her later tonight at the event.

"Now what?" Charlotte asked as she appeared in the passenger seat beside me.

She wasn't wasting any time in claiming her spot at the front of the car.

"I don't know. We have some free time before the event tonight."

"I know what we should do," Charlotte said.

"What's that?"

I knew by the look in her eyes that she was up to something.

"We should visit Ramon's wife. I'd love to hear what she has to say."

"That's an excellent idea," Maureen said.

I looked in the rearview mirror at Ramon.

He shook his head. "No way. I don't think that's a good idea at all."

"Don't you want to see your wife?" Charlotte asked.

"Not really," Ramon said.

"Oh." Charlotte pursed her lips.

"I think Ramon has something to hide that he doesn't want us to find out," Maureen said.

"And if we talk to his wife, we will find out what it is," Charlotte said.

I had to agree with them.

"Ramon, why don't you want me to talk with your wife? It may help with finding your killer. Don't you want the person responsible for this to be behind bars?" I asked.

He sighed. "Yes, I do, but just don't believe everything she says."

I looked at Charlotte again. She quirked an eyebrow.

"That means believe everything she says."

I bit back a laugh. "Okay, tell me where to go."

"You need to turn around. It's in the opposite direction."

I made a turnaround in a McDonald's parking lot and headed in the opposite direction.

"How far is it?" I asked.

"About thirty minutes."

"Why is everything so spread out?" I asked.

"It's a big city."

"You're used to a small town," Charlotte said.

"Yeah, I guess you're right," I said.

Chapter 15

Grandma Pearl's Pearls of Wisdom

*There's a new day tomorrow,
and it hasn't been touched yet.*

We arrived at an upscale subdivision. Large stone signs welcomed us to Stonebridge Estates. Shade trees lined the streets, and sprinklers pirouetted across the green, carpet-like lawns.

"It's the second street on the right, fifth house on the left."

I made the second right and counted down to the house.

"It's a beautiful house, Ramon," Maureen said.

The house looked as if it was only a couple of years old. It was big, with a brick and stone façade.

"We just moved in about a year ago," Ramon said. "I suppose my wife will have to move out now."

"Probably not," Charlotte said. "I guess you had a nice hunk of insurance that would pay the house off, right? If not, that's bad financial planning on your part."

Charlotte, always the businesswoman.

"I did have an insurance policy. My wife was the beneficiary."

"Uh huh," Charlotte said with a click of her tongue.

I knew what Charlotte was thinking. Had his wife killed him for the money? I walked up the flower-lined path to the front door and rang the doorbell. The entry was huge and made me feel small and slightly intimidated about what I was about to do. Wouldn't Kristina be surprised to know that I was standing on the front porch with the ghost of her dead husband?

"I suppose I could go on in. After all, it was my house," Ramon said with a laugh.

Only a few seconds passed until the front door was opened. It was Ramon's wife, Kristina. She looked me up and down as if she recognized me. Her dark hair fell past her shoulders in the same style as when I'd first seen her. A form-fitting black tank top and a pair of skinny jeans was her outfit today. Delicate pearl earrings dotted her earlobes in contrast to her casual clothing.

"Good afternoon, Ms. Gooden. My name is Cookie Chanel. I wondered if I could talk to you about your husband?"

"Do I know you?" she snapped.

"I don't think you're going to get past the gate-keeper," Maureen said.

"I work with the owner of the horse your husband was going to ride in the Derby."

"Good thinking, Cookie," Charlotte said.

Kristina quirked an eyebrow, as if she wondered why the heck I would want to talk with her.

She stepped out of the way and gestured. "Come inside."

That was easier than I thought. I stepped into the house and gazed up at the grand double-sided spiral staircase. Kristina motioned toward the room on the right as if she didn't want me to linger in the hallway too long.

"We can sit in here."

The room was decorated in black and white. White chairs were placed in front of the fireplace, along with a black and white striped sofa.

"This seems like something you'd like," Charlotte said. "Very fortics glam."

Charlotte sat in the white chair in front of the fireplace. She crossed her legs and placed her hands on her lap. Kristina walked over and sat on top of Charlotte. Charlotte let out a scream and jumped up.

Kristina had the funniest look on her face, as if she'd sensed something.

"I feel so violated," Charlotte said as she dashed across the room.

She should watch where she's sitting. I sat on the sofa. I was almost afraid to sit down and mess up the lovely room. Kristina started talking before I even asked any questions. Technically, she didn't even know why I was there other than to talk about Ramon. I could have wanted anything.

Kristina shook her head. "He was cheating on me."

"Oh boy," Maureen said.

"Maybe I should wait in the car," Ramon said.

"Sit down and listen." Charlotte barked the order.

Ramon didn't listen to Charlotte and disappeared. She would let him have it later. Whatever Kristina was about to tell us must be bad.

"He was cheating? How do you know this?" I asked.

Kristina stared me straight in the eyes and said, "I have video proof."

"Oh boy," Charlotte said.

"Can we see?" Maureen asked.

I glared at her when Kristina wasn't looking. I really didn't think that was a video I wanted to watch.

"I can show it to you, if you'd like," Kristina offered.

"Yes!" Maureen said.

"That really won't be necessary," I said.

Watching such a video hardly sounded enjoyable to me.

"Sometimes Cookie spoils all the fun." Charlotte leaned in for a closer look at a picture on the mantel. "Look at this photo. I think she cut Ramon's face out."

I wished I could get a closer look at that.

"Who was he cheating with?" I asked. "Do you know this person?"

"Oh, I know her all right. She's one of the lowest life forms on this planet."

"Now I'm dying to know who it is." Charlotte laughed. "Dying? Get it?"

Maureen laughed. "Good one, Charlotte."

They were hardly helping the situation. It was hard to concentrate on the conversation with their antics.

"Who is it?" I pressed.

The anticipation was getting to me too.

"Tell us!" Charlotte said.

"Mandy Neville. She's the trainer of the horse. I assume you know her."

"Wow, so they were having an affair after all," Charlotte said.

"That gives Kristina more than one motive for the murder," Maureen said.

"Or Mandy," Charlotte said.

All I could think about was the fact that I was sitting in the living room of a potential murderer, and I had talked with Mandy earlier, though Mandy had blamed Danielle. I didn't know what to think. Either way, it was scary.

I cleared my throat. "So, um, how did you catch them on this video?"

"It was easy. I just followed them. They weren't exactly good at hiding what they were doing. I think Mandy actually wanted people to know. She's a sociopath."

"What did she do that made you suspicious?"

"Well, like I said, they didn't try to hide it. The horse community is a tight one. Word spreads quickly, and it didn't take long for the rumors to get to me."

In the distance, a phone rang.

"Will you excuse me?" Kristina stood from the chair.

"Absolutely," I said with a smile.

"I'm getting a strange vibe from her," Charlotte said.

"Psst. Psst."

I looked around to see where the noise was coming from. Ramon was peeking around the corner from the front hallway.

"What are you doing?" I whispered.

"Is it safe to come in?"

"Based on what your ex-wife just told us, I'd say not." Charlotte glowered at Ramon.

"Where is she?" Ramon inched into the room.

"She went to answer the phone. You have some explaining to do."

Charlotte, Maureen, and I glared at him.

"Tell her this, 'Come on, you know he loved you. Mandy meant nothing to him. It will never happen again . . .' er, well, leave the last part out."

I stared at him with my mouth dropped open. "You actually think that will work?"

He looked at me, confused. "What's wrong with it?"

"It doesn't sound sincere, and that's what all cheaters say."

Ramon walked over to the hallway and peeked out, watching for Kristina.

"Well, at the very least, you can ask her if she killed me."

"Are you kidding me? I can't just come out and ask her if she murdered someone."

"Excuse me?" Kristina asked.

I looked over and spotted her standing in the doorway. She scowled. How would I explain myself out of this one?

"I was singing a song," I said.

Charlotte groaned.

"Just change the subject quickly, and she'll forget about it," Maureen said.

I'd follow her advice. That was all I had.

"I can understand how you felt about what Ramon did."

Kristina stared before crossing the room. I held my breath, wondering if she was coming over to kick me out. Instead, she sat down again.

"Whew, that was a close one." Maureen wiped her forehead as if she'd been sweating.

Kristina leaned forward in her chair, "I can't tell you how angry I was . . . but mostly I was angry at him. He betrayed me. I would expect something like that from Mandy. I expected much more from Ramon."

The look in her eyes had changed. A darkness overcame them, and a blank look settled in, as if she was tuning out. She was still sitting there with me talking, but she was actually somewhere else. Was she replaying the murder in her mind?

"I think it's about time that we leave, Cookie." Charlotte stood from the chair and motioned for me to follow her to the door.

If Charlotte was disturbed by someone's behavior, then I knew that I'd better take her advice.

I pushed to my feet. "Thanks for talking with me."

I hurried toward the door. Before I reached it, Kristina stopped in front of me. Her eyes were locked on my face. Her expression looked even darker now.

"This doesn't look good, Cookie. I'm nervous. You have to get out of here," Charlotte said.

She didn't have to tell me. I wanted to leave in the worst way. Currently, Kristina was blocking the door, making that impossible.

"Thanks again for talking to me. I really should be leaving now." I tried to move around her.

She blocked me again.

"Push her down. Knock her out if you have to." Maureen pumped her fist as if she was ready for a fight.

"Don't hurt her," Ramon pleaded.

Kristina stared at me. "Did Mandy send you here?"

"No, absolutely not," I said. "I'm just trying to find out who killed your husband for the horse's owner. He's concerned, that's all."

That was a complete lie. Well, for all I knew, the

owner was concerned, but he certainly hadn't asked me to find the killer. That was all me.

Her stance eased.

"Whew. It looks like she believes you," Charlotte said.

Kristina stepped away from the door. "I'm sorry if I was suspicious. You can understand, right?"

"Absolutely," I said, moving closer to the door.

"Are you sure you wouldn't like to stay for dinner?" Kristina asked.

"Thanks for the offer. I need to go."

"She never made dinner for me," Ramon said.

"Maybe I've said too much." She looked at me for a reaction.

Were those tears in her eyes?

Charlotte tapped her Prada-covered foot against the floor. "Oh, she said too much all right, but it's a little late to take that back."

"I feel so bad for what I did to her." Ramon stepped over to Kristina. He reached out to touch her, but of course his hand went straight through her arm.

"You should feel bad," Charlotte said as she moved through the front door.

"Thanks again for talking with me," I said as I opened the door and hurried outside.

"She's still watching you," Maureen said. I figured as much, but I didn't want to turn around to see.

I climbed behind the wheel of my car and took off.

"Are you going to tell the police?" Charlotte asked.

"What? My wife would never kill me," Ramon said.

"Are you sure about that?" Charlotte quirked an eyebrow.

He paused. "Well, I guess I can't be sure. She did seem mad about the affair."

"I can't believe you cheated, Ramon. What were you thinking?" I asked as I made the next left turn.

"Wow, you're a real scumbag, Ramon," Maureen said.

I wasn't going to disagree with her.

"Ramon, did your wedding vows mean nothing to you?" Charlotte asked.

"I guess I couldn't help myself. It was as if I was transfixed by Mandy. Like she had some kind of power over me. It was like witchcraft," Ramon said with a wave of his hand.

"Oh, there is no such thing." Maureen rubbed her head as if she'd developed a headache.

"Don't let Heather hear you say that," I said. "What exactly do you mean, Ramon?" I looked at him in the rearview mirror.

"Just that I couldn't resist her. She is bewitching."

Charlotte rolled her eyes.

"Cookie, look out—that truck!" Charlotte yelled.

Maureen screamed, and Ramon cursed at the truck.

I swerved and managed to avoid the truck that

had pulled out in front of me. It was the same truck that had pulled out in front of me before. I was almost sure of it. Sure, there were a lot of trucks around, but what were the odds that I would run into the same kind three times?

"I think the driver of that truck is trying to cause you to have some kind of accident," Charlotte said.

I made a quick right turn just in case the truck was really out for me. I sped down the street until I came to the on ramp for the highway.

I peeked in the rearview mirror. "Do you think the truck is back there?"

"I think you're safe . . . for now," Charlotte said.

"Do you think that person has been following you?" Maureen asked.

"It seems that way, doesn't it?"

I couldn't help but be on high alert during the entire drive back to the bed-and-breakfast. Luckily, I didn't see the truck. I had a sinking feeling in my stomach that I would see it again. When I pulled up to the bed-and-breakfast, there was another car in the driveway.

"It looks like she has another guest," Ramon said as we got out of the car.

"Good. Maybe that will keep her from worrying about what time Cookie comes back at night," Maureen said.

I locked my car and walked by the little red rental car that was parked in the driveway.

"I wonder whose it is?" Charlotte asked.

"I guess we'll find out," I said.

As soon as I walked in the door, I saw him.

A huge smile covered Ken Harrison's face. His blue eyes sparkled. He was dressed in casual tan pants and a blue shirt.

"Cookie, I'm so happy to see you." He hurried over and wrapped his arms around me.

"Oh boy. I didn't expect this," Charlotte said.

"Who is that?" Ramon asked.

"That's the other guy who has a thing for Cookie."

"Well, isn't she popular?" Ramon said.

After a couple of seconds in an embrace, I stepped back from Ken. "What are you doing here?"

"I thought I'd come to the Derby too."

I quirked an eyebrow. "Be honest. You never mentioned wanting to come to the Derby."

He smiled sheepishly. "Okay, I heard what happened, and I was worried about you."

"He probably thinks you're going to need legal advice," Charlotte said.

"Two handsome men fighting over her?" Maureen said.

They weren't fighting over me.

Ken placed his hand on my arm. "I thought I'd come down and check on you."

His eyes locked me in a gaze, and I was acutely aware of his gentle touch.

"He could have done that with a phone call," Charlotte said.

"Really, I'm fine," I said.

"Well, I wanted to see that for myself," Ken said.

"Are you staying for the Derby?" I asked.

"Yes, I thought I would since I'm here."

"Where are you staying?" I leaned against the wall, trying to act casual.

He smiled. "Right here."

"Right where?" I asked.

"At this bed-and-breakfast." Ken leaned against the small table beside him. A figurine wobbled, and he quickly grabbed and steadied the porcelain knickknack.

Charlotte chuckled. "Oh, this will be interesting."

Hannah stepped into the foyer.

"I see you met our new guest." Hannah smiled at Ken.

He hadn't told her that he knew me.

"I made dinner." Hannah eyed me up and down. "I suppose you can eat with us if you'd like, Cookie."

She didn't sound excited about that prospect.

"Oh, that's okay," I said.

"You have to eat dinner with me," Ken said with a smile. "Come on. It's a lovely evening, and we can eat outside."

"I don't know."

He grabbed my hand. "I insist."

"I just need to check on Wind Song. I'll be right back."

Ken offered a smile. "Take your time."

I ran up and added food and water to Wind Song's dishes. Grandma Pearl wasn't showing any signs of wanting to use the Ouija board or the tarot cards, so I went back downstairs. Ken and Hannah were waiting for me in the kitchen.

"I guess they wanted to make sure you didn't leave," Charlotte said.

Hannah sighed when she saw me. I wasn't sure if that was to let me know I'd taken too long or if she was actually sad that I'd returned. I followed Ken and Hannah outside and over to the picnic table. We were surrounded by rosebushes and other flowers. Their perfume drifted across to us on the breeze. Lights draped overhead from the trellis. Branches on the nearby trees stirred, rustling the leaves. The last rays of the sunset faded to a navy blue across the sky. Dylan would wonder where I was. I suppose I could have a quick dinner before going to meet him.

"Cookie, you sit on that side, and Ken can sit here beside me." Hannah pointed to the chairs.

Ken smiled and sat where he was told. I sat across from him.

"I'll be right back with the food," she said as she hurried away.

"I'm sorry if I surprised you like this," Ken said.

"That's okay. I'm doing fine, honest."

"So tell me what happened." Ken looked me in the eyes.

"I found the man in a hallway in the Kentucky Derby Museum at Churchill Downs. He'd been murdered."

"What have the police said?" he asked.

"Not much actually. I'm trying to find out more from them."

"I can ask for more info if you'd like."

"Tell him yes." Ramon gestured with his hands to reinforce his point.

What did I have to lose? The more people on the case, the faster we might solve it.

"That would be great. It's so sweet of you to offer," I said.

"Ken is a sweet guy," Charlotte said, looking at Maureen.

Maureen leaned down close to Ken's face. "Lovely smile too."

"What do you know so far?" Ken asked.

"A lot of people are accusing each other. Oh, and Ramon was having an affair." Ramon shrugged when I said that. "His wife knew about it."

"So that gives her a motive," Ken said.

I swatted at a mosquito. "She seems extremely angry."

"Rightfully so." Charlotte scowled at Ramon.

Charlotte had been cheated on in the past, so that was a sore spot for her. Before we could finish the discussion, Hannah returned with the food. She had cheeseburgers and fries. A picnic under the stars.

She set the tray on the table. "I hope you're hungry."

Ken reached out and grabbed a plate, placing it in front of me.

"I'm starving. What about you, Cookie?" he asked with a wink.

My nerves were definitely getting in the way of my appetite. I'd try my best to eat though.

"Looks delicious. Thank you." I reached for a french fry.

Hannah sat next to Ken and immediately asked him questions.

"Ken's a lawyer," she said and looked at me.

I took a bite to avoid talking.

"She has no idea that you know each other. That's funny," Charlotte said.

The dinner conversation consisted of lots of questions directed toward Ken. He took it in stride though and never acted as if he was sick of answering. Darkness had completely engulfed us now. Stars twinkled above, and fireflies lit up the air around us.

"Let me help you with the dishes," Ken said.

I grabbed a couple of plates and followed behind them toward the kitchen. Dylan would be wondering where I was. I had to leave soon. Plus, I still had to dress for the event. What would Dylan say when he arrived and saw Ken? I would just have to meet Dylan outside so he wouldn't see Ken. Better yet, maybe I could just sneak out. That way I wouldn't have a curfew. No one would know, right?

I yawned as I placed the dishes in the dishwasher.

"You must have had a long day," Ken said. "I'm tired too after the long drive."

Hannah wiped her hands on the dish towel. "Well, it's time for bed anyway."

I looked at the clock. It was now eight.

"You only have thirty minutes to get ready," Charlotte said as she paced across the floor.

She wasn't helping with my nerves. Ken walked me up to my door.

"Hannah probably won't like it if she sees you standing here with me," I said.

Ken laughed. "That's a chance I'm willing to take."

He stared at me.

"Perhaps we should give them some alone time." Ramon motioned for Charlotte and Maureen to follow him.

"Quiet, Ramon. I don't want to miss this," Charlotte said with a wave of her hand. "Cookie's life is turning into an episode of *The Bachelorette*."

"What's *The Bachelorette*?" Maureen asked.

"Reality TV," Charlotte answered quickly.

I twisted the doorknob. "Well, good night."

I felt terrible about not telling him the truth. I hadn't exactly lied, but I'd left out a lot of details.

"Good night," he said with a smile.

I hurried into my room and grabbed my dress.

Chapter 16

Cookie's Savvy Tips for Vintage Shopping

*If you're looking for something in particular,
don't be afraid to ask the sales associate
for help. You can request a piece,
and the shop owner might find it for you.*

My Vicky Tiel gray, lace-covered gown was
from the eighties. Sparkling beads and sequins
covered the lace. It had short sleeves and a boat
neckline. After spritzing Chanel perfume along
my neck and wrists, I eased my room door open.
Peeking out to the left and right, I saw no one was
in the hallway.

The old floor squeaked with almost every foot-
step. I wasn't sure how I would manage to sneak
out with that kind of noise. Anxiety had settled in
my stomach. I was an adult and free to do whatever I wanted as long as it was legal. Going to this
party was legal. So why was I so worried? After
taking another deep breath and exhaling, I tiptoed

out of the room. I eased the door shut behind me.
I tiptoed across the floor. The floor squeaked, and
I froze.

"Shhh," Charlotte said.

My heart beat faster as I took another couple of
steps. So far, so good. The ghosts tiptoed behind
me, as if they would make noise too. I suppose it
was possible. People heard noises in haunted
houses all the time.

I reached the stairs. My leg muscles burned
from trying to tiptoe so much. The second-to-last
stair tread made a loud moan. Luckily, I didn't
think it was as audible at the top of the stairs. I
raced over to the front door and rushed outside.
Good thing my landlady didn't have an alarm.
Headlights turned into the drive. The light briefly
blinded me. I hoped the light didn't flash into the
windows and alert anyone.

As soon as Dylan pulled up, I hurried over to
the car and jumped in the passenger seat. I didn't
give him time to get out and hold the door open
for me.

"Are we running late?" Dylan asked with a
chuckle.

I laughed nervously. "I guess I'm just anxious
to get there."

When he pulled out onto the road, I released my
pent-up breath.

"You look beautiful," Dylan said.

"Thank you." I smiled.

A chorus of *aww* came from the backseat. Now
I had to worry about how I was going to get back

in the house in a few hours. I took a look at what Dylan was wearing for the first time.

"Wow, you're wearing a tuxedo," I said.

"Black tie event, right?" He glanced at me.

"Yes, it's just that you look so handsome."

He smiled as he kept his eyes on the road. "Thank you."

We made the drive shorter by taking the highway, zipping past traffic and into the outer edges of town. When we pulled up to the house, I couldn't help but stare. A mixture of stone and brick covered the façade for an old-world look. Extensive landscaping of cedar trees, shrubs, and perennial flowers decorated the front, welcoming guests.

"It's huge. I'd hate to have to clean all the rooms in this place."

"I'm sure they have someone to help with that." Dylan parked the car and turned off the ignition. "Are you ready to go in?"

I continued to stare at the house. "I've never been a fan of these kind of events."

"What?" Charlotte asked loudly from the backseat. "How could you not like a party like this?"

She should know by now that I liked a quieter, more laid-back event.

"You know, we don't have to stay," Dylan said.

I looked at him. "No, I want to go."

"I'm not too convinced," he said.

I opened the car door. "It'll be fun." I forced a smile.

Dylan climbed out of the car. He held my hand as we walked down the sidewalk toward the house.

At least I didn't have to go to this party alone. Lights lined the path, casting a dazzling glow over the landscaping. A fountain bubbled somewhere nearby. When we reached the house, I pulled the invitation from my bag and handed it to the man standing guard at the front door.

The tall, muscular man looked at the paper. Next, he eyed us up and down. "Identification, please."

After we provided our credentials, the guy allowed us past the roped-off section. We hadn't even made it to the front door when Dylan's phone rang.

He looked at the number and said, "I really need to take this call."

"Sure. Go ahead."

Dylan and I stepped over to the side of the walkway so he could answer.

"Detective Valentine," he said.

The ghosts and I listened to his side of the conversation.

"Interesting. Okay, thanks for letting me know." Dylan met my gaze after clicking off the call.

"What's interesting?" Charlotte asked.

The ghosts stood close to Dylan. What would he think if he knew?

"That was my source."

"You have a source?" I asked.

He shrugged. "I guess you could say that."

"What did your source tell you?"

"He said that Ramon was poisoned."

My eyes widened.

"Poisoned?" Charlotte, Maureen, Ramon, and I said "poisoned" at the same time.

We were all stunned.

"Yes, that's what he said," Dylan said.

"That's terrible," I said.

"Apparently, his body had a high dose of a drug that is normally given to horses."

"Would he have taken something like that? Maybe this wasn't murder after all."

"It would be a heck of a way to go," Dylan said. "And why there in that hallway?"

"I would never kill myself. I had too much to live for," Ramon said. "Besides, if I was going to do it, I surely wouldn't do it that way. I'd pick something much quicker. Who wants to suffer?"

Dylan technically never mentioned anything about suffering. Maybe Ramon was starting to re-member more and would be able to recall whether he encountered anyone in the hallway. I wanted to ask Ramon if he remembered anyone giving him something to eat or drink that tasted strange. I would have to wait until we were alone. At least Dylan had been able to discover this important information.

"We have to find out who would have access to that drug," I said.

Charlotte placed her hands on her hips. "Just about every person that Ramon came into contact with."

Yeah, she was right about that. But I didn't want to think it would be impossible to find who had given him the poison—it was all that I had to go on right now.

"Finding out who had access might be difficult," Dylan said while taking my hand into his.

"I guess we need to figure out how this person gave Ramon the drug," I said.

Dylan probably didn't have the heart to tell me that was nearly impossible. My phone rang. Who would call me? I didn't have a source. Danielle's number popped up on the screen. She was probably wondering where I was.

"Do you need to take that call?" Dylan asked.

"It's Danielle. She's the one who invited me to this party."

"You'd better talk to her," Dylan said.

I answered the call.

"Cookie, where are you?" Her voice sounded strained.

"I'm right outside of the party," I said, looking up at the giant house.

"I was afraid of that," she said. "I can't make it, but you go ahead and have a great time. I'll call you in the morning."

I debated whether I should tell her about the poison. Ultimately, I decided to wait since Dylan hadn't told me if I could share the information.

"See you tomorrow," I said.

"Is everything okay?" Dylan asked.

I placed the phone in my purse. "That was Danielle. She can't make it to the party."

"Let's get out of here," Dylan said.

"What do you mean?" I asked.

"We don't have to stay if she isn't coming."

"We don't?"

"You don't even want to be here. So let's go somewhere else." Dylan's lips slipped into a charming grin.

"That's so romantic," Charlotte said dreamily.

I smiled. "Where are we going?"

Dylan held my hand as we walked back to the car. "Wherever the car takes us."

"That sounds like a plan," Maureen said.

We ended up downtown in the city by the Ohio River. A large walking bridge spanned the river from Louisville to Indiana. It provided a beautiful view of the city lights. A breeze drifted in from the water, and the stars dazzled in the black sky. Lights from the skyscrapers shimmered and danced across the water. I couldn't believe that the ghosts had waited by the car. Charlotte insisted that we have a romantic walk alone.

"Are you glad I came?" Dylan asked as we walked along hand in hand.

"Of course I'm glad you came," I said. "And it's not just because you're helping me find information about the case."

"The thought had crossed my mind," he said with a smile.

Dylan and I discussed the nighttime city view with sparkling lights from the skyscrapers, the Derby, being away from Sugar Creek, and just about everything else. Time had slipped away. Forty minutes had passed, and I figured the ghosts were getting anxious. We headed back toward the car to leave. That was when I spotted a truck pulling out of the parking area. It looked exactly like the truck I'd seen before.

"Did you see that truck?" I pointed.

"I saw a black one just leave," Dylan said.

"I think that truck was following me."

"What makes you think that?" he asked.

"I saw one just like it a couple times. It pulled out in front of me and almost caused me to have a wreck. I don't think that's a coincidence," I said.

Dylan looked concerned. He wanted to keep me safe, and now there was nothing he could do about the truck.

"We'll have to keep an eye out for it." Dylan gave my hand a gentle, reassuring squeeze.

When we reached the car, the ghosts were leaning against it. They looked thoroughly bored. I wanted to ask them if they had seen the truck and what it was doing there. I would have to wait until we got back to the bed-and-breakfast. They weren't mentioning it, so I assumed they hadn't seen it.

As we pulled out onto the road, I looked in the side mirror for any sign of the truck. Headlights caught my attention, but I had no way to know if it was the truck until we got closer to the streetlight.

Dylan noticed my watching. "Is something bothering you? You look like the bogeyman is after us."

"Tell him he just might be," Charlotte said from the backseat.

I attempted a smile. "Just watching the traffic behind us."

Luckily, there was no sign of the truck. Soon we arrived back at the bed-and-breakfast. I wouldn't be able to explain why I wanted him to turn off the headlights. He pulled up in front of the house. The place was quiet, and the lights were off.

After Dylan walked me to the door and kissed me good night, I had to sneak back in the house. Dylan stood at the bottom of the steps, waiting for me to open the door and go inside. What if Hannah had locked it, and I had to ring the doorbell? Sleeping outside in my car might be a better option.

I eased the door open as quietly as I could without making Dylan notice that I was being so careful. I waved good-bye and closed the door. Now that the door was shut, I leaned my back against it and released a deep breath. The stress wasn't over yet. I had to get back up those stairs.

As I moved across the foyer toward the stairs, a movement caught my attention. I thought for sure I heard the floor squeak upstairs. When I glanced up, I thought I saw Ken peering down from the second floor. The movement had been so quick, though, that I wasn't sure. Was he awake? Did he know that I had been out? I eased up the first two steps. They squeaked loudly, and I froze. After a few seconds, I knew I had to move again. I couldn't stand on the stairs for the rest of the night. Easing my foot onto the next step, I released a deep breath when it made no noise. I had to push through or this would take all night. After holding my breath the entire way up the stairs, I made it to the top.

"You're not very good at sneaking around," Charlotte said.

"I made it, didn't I?" I whispered.

I looked around to see if the other room doors were closed. It looked as if I'd successfully snuck in, though I was fairly certain that Ken had been awake when I first came in. I hoped that he hadn't seen me. I guess I'd find out in the morning if he asked me.

Once inside my room, I had a chance to ask Ramon what I'd wanted to all evening.

"Ramon, do you remember drinking something that tasted strange? Did someone put something in your drink?"

"Don't you think if he remembered that he would have told you by now?" Charlotte placed her hands on her hips.

"It doesn't hurt to ask," I said.

"I'll try to remember," Ramon stood by the window and peered out into the night. He made no reflection in the window.

Chapter 17

Grandma Pearl's Pearls of Wisdom

*I'd rather be someone's shot of whiskey
than be everyone's cup of tea.*

The sun streamed through the window the next morning.

"Rise and shine, princess," Charlotte said as she stood next to the bed, peering down at me.

"Must you do that?" I asked.

"We have work to do. Get up." She managed to move the covers slightly.

I groaned and shuffled out of bed. For today's outfit, I'd selected a Pauline Trigère pink pin-striped sleeveless dress. It had a darted bust, a fitted waist, and an ultra-full accordion-pleated skirt. Instead of high heels, I wore a pair of white wedge-heeled flip-flops. I wanted to be super casual but still look put together. That was no easy task.

Charlotte was in her typical high-fashion style,

wearing a pair of J Brand high-waist dark blue slacks with a white and blue striped cold shoulder silk blouse. Her shoes were Christian Louboutin, of course. She looked like a million bucks. Maureen wore a light blue short-sleeved dress with black pumps. She said she'd made the dress. Of course, all the ghosts had to do was think of an outfit and it appeared. I assumed she'd made the dress years ago. It was seven-thirty, and I figured Hannah had breakfast ready and was probably waiting for me. I wondered if Ken was awake.

I peeked out the window but didn't see his car. Had he gone somewhere already this morning? After I showered and dressed, I opened the door and stepped out into the hallway. When I turned around, Hannah was right behind me.

I jumped. "Oh, I didn't see you there."

She placed her hands on her hips. "I know what you did last night."

"Uh-oh. I told you that you were bad at sneaking around," Charlotte said.

"She'll probably kick you out," Maureen said.

"Excuse me?" I asked, trying to pretend as if I didn't know what she meant.

"I heard you moving around in the hallway, and I know what you were doing."

"I can explain," I said.

She held her hand up. "No need."

"Yeah, she's going to kick her out now," Charlotte said.

"This is interesting to watch," Maureen said.

"You were trying to get into the attic to see all the vintage clothing I have up there."

"What?" Charlotte asked.

Maureen laughed.

"I didn't see that coming," Ramon said.

"You'd better just agree with her," Charlotte said. "It's better than her thinking you slipped out with Dylan."

How would I even know that she had vintage clothing up there, other than the fact that people sometimes kept old things in attics?

"I just wanted a little peek," I said.

"Good job, Cookie," Charlotte said.

"Well, you should have asked. I would have shown you." Her voice was full of agitation.

"I didn't think you'd show me."

"Way to go along with it, Cookie," Maureen said.

"I can show you now if you'd like."

I was surprised that she was offering.

"Okay," I said.

"She is an odd duck," Charlotte said.

"Follow me to the attic." Hannah motioned over her shoulder.

"Attics are creepy," Charlotte said.

Yes, attics were creepy, but I'd spent my share of time in them, searching for vintage pieces. I followed Hannah across the hallway. She pulled the ladder down and motioned for me to go first.

"What if she locks you in there?" Charlotte asked.

I hadn't thought of that until she mentioned it. Now I was nervous. I hesitated, and Hannah motioned for me to go ahead. I hoped that the ghosts would get help for me if she did lock me in there. What was I thinking? Hannah seemed nice enough, except for the curfew thing. She wouldn't really lock me in the attic, right? After releasing a deep breath, I started climbing. I peeked over my shoulder a couple of times to see if she was coming too. So far, she was behind me.

I reached the top and stepped into the cramped, dimly lit space. A bit of sunshine came through the small window on the other side of the room. Dust motes drifted through the air like shimmering snowflakes. It was early May, but it had already started to warm up in the space, though it wasn't too bad. Thank goodness Hannah had come up there with me. I wouldn't let her lock me up here now.

"I have the stuff right over here in this trunk," she said as she walked across the space.

I followed her over to the corner of the room. She pulled out a key from her pocket and unlocked an old beat-up trunk. A loud groan of the hinges filled the room when she opened the lid. I peeked over her shoulder at the contents. It was full of clothing and even some hats.

"This place reminds me of my home," Maureen said, looking around the space.

"You can take a look at the stuff, but you can't have it." Hannah warned with a wiggle of her finger.

I grabbed for the clothing. If I found a real treasure, maybe I could convince her to let me buy it. After digging through the items like a dog looking for a bone, my enthusiasm waned. Unfortunately, there wasn't much in the trunk that I couldn't live without. It was mainly suits from the seventies and pants and tops from the eighties. Nothing special. But when I spotted the white silk dress at the bottom of the trunk, my stomach danced. It looked like a wedding gown.

I pulled the dress from the trunk. It was in surprisingly good condition, considering it had been stuffed in this wooden box. The body was a silhouette skirt with a sweep train. The silk underlay was covered with floral lace around the bodice. The taffeta sash was tied into a large bow in the back.

"This is amazing," I said, touching the lace-covered buttons. "Where did you get it?"

I guessed the date was from the early 1920s. She should have this dress displayed as art.

"It was my grandmother's dress. I just never knew what to do with it. It looks like it would fit you. Why don't you try it on?"

"Oh no, I couldn't," I said, though I was tempted.

She shoved the dress toward me. "No, I insist. I can tell you love it."

I was curious about how the dress would look.

"I will look away while you change," Hannah said. "You can undress right here."

Ramon didn't budge. Charlotte lured him away so that I could slip into the gown. After taking off my dress, I pulled on the wedding gown, though the back was still undone.

"How does it look?" I asked.

Hannah gasped. "It looks stunning."

She moved around to the back. "Let me button it for you."

Once she finished, she moved across the room and pulled a sheet off something in the corner. It was a full-length mirror. I looked at my reflection. The dress was even more beautiful than I had thought. The fabric fell in all the right places.

Charlotte gasped when she saw me. "Cookie, it is perfect."

"You will make a gorgeous bride," Maureen said.

Except I had no plans for marriage in the near future. That was kind of important in order for me to be a bride. I hadn't really thought about a wedding gown or what type of wedding I might want.

"Here, hold these fake roses." Hannah had pulled them from a box.

I held the roses in front of me and studied my reflection. Hannah hummed the bridal march. Movement caught my attention. When I glanced over, I spotted Ken. He stared at me.

"Oh, great. The poor guy will think you are planning a wedding," Ramon said.

"No dating advice from you," Charlotte warned him.

I tossed the roses onto the floor. "Hannah had some vintage clothing, so they talked me into trying on the dress."

"You just said 'they,' Cookie," Charlotte warned.

I'd been so flustered that I didn't know what I was saying.

"They?" He quirked an eyebrow.

"I mean 'she'." I knew my cheeks were red since I felt the heat on my face.

Ken stepped closer to us. "I thought I heard voices up here. By the way, I think you look beautiful."

"I think he's getting ideas," Charlotte said.

"Don't do it, guy. Run the other way." Ramon motioned toward the ladder.

"Oh, be quiet," Charlotte said.

"I'll just get out of this dress," I said.

"We'll wait for you downstairs," Hannah said, looping her arm through Ken's.

When they climbed down the stairs, I slipped out of the dress.

"That was embarrassing," I whispered.

"He had hearts in his eyes when he saw you," Maureen said.

"Cookie, you have a real dilemma on your hands," Charlotte said.

"What's that?" I asked.

"Dylan or Ken? Which one will you pick?"

"I'm dating Dylan. There is no picking," I said, stepping into my other dress.

"But you have feelings for Ken. I can see it in your eyes," Maureen said, pointing at me.

"Ken is a nice man. I enjoy his friendship," I said, checking my reflection in the mirror.

"Is everything okay up there?" Ken called out.

I moved over to the stairs and climbed down.

"Just fine," I said with a smile when I reached the bottom.

"I thought you might have gotten lost in all those boxes." Ken helped me down the last step.

I pushed the hair out of my eyes. "I thought you'd left."

"What makes you think that?" Ken asked.

"I didn't see your car this morning." I studied his face.

Would he mention seeing me sneak in last night?

"I decided to go for a ride. It was such a beautiful morning. I would have asked you to go, but I figured you wouldn't want to since you came home late."

Okay, so he had seen me.

"You don't have to explain anything to him," Maureen said.

"She owes it to the guy," Ramon said.

"No, she doesn't." Charlotte frowned.

"Maybe tomorrow morning," I offered.

"I'd like that," Ken said. "Are you busy now? I was thinking about doing some sightseeing."

"That's a tough one to answer," Charlotte said.

"Can I get back to you on that? I'm not sure about my plans."

A look of disappointment took over his face. "You know how to reach me."

Ken turned and walked toward his room.

"That's a bummer for him," Ramon said.

Chapter 18

Cookie's Savvy Tips for Vintage Shopping

*It's best to measure a garment rather than go by
sizing since it has changed over the years.*

I had to find out who had access to the drug.
Charlotte, Maureen, and Ramon all agreed that it
would be impossible, but what other option did I
have? So I decided I'd go to the backside and look
around. Maybe I could talk to a few people. It was
worth a try. Dylan had no idea that I was going. I
suppose I could have used his help; after all, he did
have detective skills. I didn't want to disturb his
sleep though. This was like a vacation for him, and
he should sleep in.

"Cookie says she wants Dylan to relax and not
have to wake up early to go with her, but I really
know she just wants to solve the case on her own,"

Charlotte said to Maureen as she turned around in the front seat. "She's competitive like that."

"I am not," I said as I steered the Buick onto the road.

Charlotte stared at me.

"Okay. I'm a little competitive, but that's a good thing. It makes me work harder."

"All work and no play." Charlotte wagged her finger in my direction.

She was one to talk. She had been the hardest worker to ever live in Sugar Creek before her untimely death. I drove across town to Churchill Downs. Luckily, the guy at the guard shack recognized my car by now and waved me on through. I parked under a shade tree and hopped out. The ghosts followed me across the parking lot like ducklings.

"Where are you going first?" Charlotte asked.

"I don't know. I guess I will just look around. If I recognize anyone, I can talk to them," I said.

"I know a lot of people. I could tell you what to say to them to start a conversation," Ramon said.

That was tempting, but I would still feel weird about doing that.

"I'll see how things go," I said.

I passed by the barn but didn't see Danielle. When I looked across the way, I spotted Mandy's truck. No one was around.

"I know what you're thinking," Charlotte said.

"What am I thinking?" I whispered so that no one would hear me.

"You want to take a look in Mandy's truck."

I bit back a smile. "Would that be such a bad thing?"

Charlotte rolled her eyes and looked at Maureen and Ramon. "Cookie wants to know if snooping around Mandy's truck would be a bad thing. What do you guys think?"

Maureen and Ramon shook their heads at the same time.

"What?" I asked. "You don't think I should do it? What could happen?"

"You're getting too brave for your own good," Ramon said.

"Mandy will snap you like a twig if she catches you messing around with her truck," Charlotte said.

I scoffed. "Never underestimate the power of Cookie Chanel."

Charlotte chuckled.

"I'll just walk over there. There's nothing wrong with going near the truck. She can't have me arrested for that."

"Don't be so sure," Ramon said. "Mandy has a way of manipulating people to get what she wants. She could convince the police you were trying to steal it."

He spoke as if from experience. Nevertheless, I decided to do it anyway. I'd take my chances. I headed over toward the truck, watching my surroundings the entire time. Strolling along, I tried to act casual. I didn't want anyone to be suspicious. If they reported me acting weird, I would be kicked out.

I couldn't believe that I was doing this. Regardless, I had to take some risks if I was going to solve this case. Charlotte was right again. Mandy was a bit scary. If Mandy discovered me looking in her truck, I had no idea how I would respond. At least the truck was parked under a tree, which would offer a bit of concealment.

When I reached the truck, I looked around once again to see if anyone was watching. Luckily, everyone was busy, and no one seemed to even notice I was around. I stepped up close to the driver's-side window.

"Just be careful," Charlotte said. "If Mandy catches you and decides to attack, make sure to go for the eyes. Poke her in the eyes."

"That sounds kind of violent, Charlotte," I said.

"You'll do what you have to do if it comes down to life or death."

I pressed my face next to the window.

"What do you see?" Charlotte asked.

"A mess," I said.

Charlotte, Maureen, and Ramon moved over to the truck too.

"Whoa. It's a pigsty in there. Ramon, did you ever ride in this car?" Maureen asked.

He shook his head. "We were always in my car."

"It's a good thing. You might have gotten lost in there," Charlotte said with a laugh. "Mandy seems as if she is three gallons of crazy in a two-gallon bucket."

I peered in. "I can't see anything for the mess. I'll have to open the door for a closer peek."

"Good luck with that. You might need a hazmat suit and face mask," Charlotte said.

I scanned the surroundings one more time before pulling on the door handle. Luckily, the door opened. Unfortunately, trash spilled out onto the ground. Oh, great.

"I don't want to touch that stuff to put it back."

"Just leave it." Charlotte rubbed her arms as if she had a shiver at the thought of touching the stuff.

"That is littering," I said.

"Mandy will get it when she comes back to her truck," Charlotte said.

"That's doubtful," Maureen said.

"She'll know that someone was looking in her truck," I said.

"She won't know that it was you." Charlotte motioned. "Now hurry up before she comes back."

I inched over to the seat and poked a few things with a tree branch I'd picked up from the ground.

"What do you see?" Charlotte asked.

The ghosts had moved away from the truck now as if it was actually a biohazard. Maybe it was, for all I knew.

"A lot of fast-food wrappers. I don't think she cooks at home much," I said.

"Totally unhealthy," Charlotte said.

"What else is in there?" Maureen asked.

"There are books. They look like journals."

"Bingo. Pull those out and have a look," Charlotte said.

"I don't know if that's a good idea." Ramon paced back and forth.

"Do you want to find your killer or not?" Charlotte placed her hands on her hips.

I had to actually reach my hand in if I wanted to pick up a book.

I blew out a deep breath. "Here goes."

I stuck my hand in and made contact with a wrapper.

"Ew." I pulled my hand out quickly.

What I hoped was mustard was now on my hand. I managed to locate a napkin on the seat. Of course, it had been used.

"You'd better hurry up," Charlotte said. "Quit goofing off."

"Does this look like I'm goofing off?" I held up my mustard-stained hand.

"Actually, yes," Charlotte said.

I sighed and made another attempt. This time I made contact with a book. After pulling it out, I saw it was a journal. I opened the cover and read the first page.

"What does it say?" Charlotte asked, now moving closer so she could peer over my shoulder.

"It's a poem, I guess."

> *Moonbeams surround me.*
> *Take away the pain.*
> *Harm anyone who dares cross.*

"That's an odd poem," I said.

"It is the worst I've ever read," Charlotte said.

"Is that even a poem?" Maureen frowned.

I flipped a couple of pages. The journal was full of similar writing.

"Don't read any more of them." Charlotte waved her hand.

A letter fell from between the pages and floated to the ground.

"Something fell out." Maureen pointed.

I reached down and picked up the piece of paper.

"What is it?" Charlotte asked.

I unfolded it. "I guess I'll find out."

"I really don't think you should be doing this," Ramon said.

I didn't understand why he was so concerned with my snooping if he really wanted me to find the killer. I had to look if I wanted to find any clues. I quickly read the paper.

"It's a letter," I said, turning to face Ramon.

"Oh, a letter to Ramon or from him?" Charlotte asked, picking up on why I was looking at Ramon.

"Is it a love letter?" Maureen asked.

"Not exactly," I said with a smirk.

"Well, tell us what it is," Charlotte said.

"Apparently, Ramon was breaking up with Mandy."

"So much for denying that you weren't having an affair," Charlotte said.

Charlotte and Maureen moved away from

Ramon. Now they were standing beside me. They eyed him up and down.

"We can't stand cheaters," Charlotte and Maureen said in unison.

"I think you've made that more than evident," Ramon said.

"How could you?" Charlotte pumped her fist in front of his face.

"So despicable." Maureen shook her head.

I would have added a comment, but they were doing a pretty good job of making him feel bad.

"Did you write this letter?" I asked.

Ramon stared at us. "Okay, so we were having an affair, but as you can see, I broke it off."

Charlotte scoffed. "As if that makes it okay?"

"No, it doesn't make it okay," he said.

"So what did she say when you gave her this letter?" I asked.

"She was upset with me," Ramon said.

"Mad enough to kill you?" Charlotte asked.

"I don't think she would do that." Ramon looked away from us.

"Look us in the eyes and say that," I said.

Ramon looked at us again. "I don't think . . . okay, maybe she could have killed me. Are you happy? I admitted it."

"Okay, enough about that," I said. "What did Mandy say?"

Ramon shrugged. "Well, needless to say, she was angry. She said I would regret breaking up with her."

"Oh, that sounds like a threat to me," Charlotte said.

"Anything else?" I asked.

"She said she would kill herself."

"It looked like maybe she changed that plan and decided to kill you instead," Maureen said.

"I still don't think she would do something like that to me."

"To be honest, Ramon, Mandy seems like an angry person. I mean, all of these poems are so negative." I waved the book.

Ramon stared at us. "Do you really think she killed me?"

"That's what we're trying to figure out," I said.

"Okay, we should get out of here unless you think there is something else to find in that truck," Charlotte said. "I'm worried that Mandy will show up. Someone could have told her that you were snooping around in her truck."

Charlotte was right. I was beginning to feel nervous about being there after reading Mandy's dark words. If there was anything else in there, I didn't think I'd find it underneath all the junk. I tossed the journal back into the car and closed the door.

"Don't you think you should put the book back where you found it?" Maureen asked.

"How would she know where anything was in that junk heap?" Charlotte said.

Maureen peeked into the truck again. "You have a valid point."

"Now come on, Cookie. Let's go before she arrives." Charlotte gestured for me to follow her.

"It's too late," Ramon said. "Here comes Mandy now."

I looked across the way and spotted Mandy. Thank goodness, she wasn't looking at me. I guess she hadn't spotted me yet. I needed to keep it that way.

"You have to hide," Charlotte said.

I took off running away from the truck in the opposite direction from Mandy. The space was wide open, and I knew Mandy might spot me. Where could I hide? I spotted a nearby giant oak tree. When I reached the tree, I hid behind it. My breathing was heavy, and my heart thumped wildly. I had to calm down.

"What is she doing?" I asked.

I didn't want to peek out for fear that she would see me.

"She's walking up to the truck. Wait, she just paused. She's looking around." Charlotte reported.

"She's looking for me, isn't she?" I asked in a panic.

"We don't know that for sure, so try to stay calm," Charlotte said.

I took in a deep breath and released it, trying to calm my nerves.

"She definitely senses something. Maybe she noticed the trash on the ground and wonders if someone opened her truck." Charlotte stood next to the tree, but not too far away from me.

"Based on the condition of her truck, I doubt she ever notices much," Maureen said.

"What is she doing now?" I asked.

"Okay, she opened her truck door and got in. Now she's leaving."

I released another deep breath. Thank goodness, she hadn't caught me. That was a close one.

Chapter 19

Grandma Pearl's Pearls of Wisdom

Just smile and wave.

After getting away from Mandy, I made my way over to the barn. I wanted to talk with Danielle, although she wasn't expecting me to show up this morning. As I approached, I heard someone using colorful language.

"Sounds as if someone is angry this morning," Charlotte said.

The ghosts and I eased down the aisle toward the sound of the voice. I was almost afraid to find out what was going on. The closer I got, the more I realized it sounded like Danielle. I hoped that everything was okay. Maybe she'd had more problems with Mandy.

When I reached the horse stall, I stopped. Danielle had a rake and was shoveling hay. The entire time, she was complaining. She didn't even realize I was standing there.

She noticed me. "Oh, Cookie. I didn't know you were coming by."

"I just thought I'd stop by and say hi. Is everything okay?" I asked.

"It sure doesn't look like everything is okay," Charlotte said.

Danielle blew the hair out of her eyes. "If anything gets done around here, I have to be the one to do it. The groom has disappeared, and now I'm stuck cleaning the stalls."

"What do you mean he's missing?" I asked.

She stepped out of the stall. "Corbin is gone. He just didn't show up for work. I guess he decided he didn't want to do this anymore. Which is kind of odd, considering he's been working for us for a long time and has never done this type of thing."

"Have you checked with friends and family? Maybe he's just sick."

Danielle brushed hay from her pants. "He lives alone, but neighbors say they saw him moving out of his place. I guess he just decided to take off. He could have at least said good-bye. He didn't give a warning or anything."

"This sounds suspicious, if you ask me," Charlotte said.

Maureen stood beside Danielle. "Do you think Corbin could be the killer? Maybe that's why he took off so quickly."

"I know Corbin, and he's a good guy," Ramon said.

"Yeah, that's what you said about Mandy too. I don't think you're a good judge of character," Charlotte said.

Charlotte had a point. Maybe Corbin did want to get out of town before the police discovered he was the killer. What was his motive though? I'd heard Mandy had had some not so nice things to say to him. But other than the fact that Mandy had been mean to him, it seemed that he'd enjoyed working at the barn.

Maybe people were wrong though. Maybe something had happened to Corbin. What if the killer had killed Corbin too?

"Do you think something has happened to him?" I asked.

She pushed a lock of blond hair out of her eyes. "I doubt it since the neighbors saw him moving."

"Is there something I can do to help?" I asked.

"Oh yeah, I can just see Cookie cleaning out a horse stall." Charlotte laughed.

Sure, it looked like hard work, but I thought I could handle the task.

"Thanks, Cookie, but I'm finished now."

"Let me know if I can help later," I said.

"You'd better hope she doesn't take you up on that," Charlotte said.

"I'll make sure to let you know." Danielle scanned the area. "I need to make a call. I'll talk to you later."

As I walked away from the barn, the ghosts started chatting.

"You need to find Corbin," Charlotte said.

"Yes, that would be great, but I'm sure the police are trying to track him down. If he truly left, he probably isn't even in Kentucky now."

"I hope he's okay," Ramon said. "Do you think if he was killed his ghost will show up too?"

"I don't know what to think about ghosts."

All ghosts couldn't appear to me, right? I hoped not because I didn't have any more space in my car. It was already crowded there. I turned the corner and bumped into a man.

"Cookie, you need to watch what you're doing when walking around here."

Olson Fine was the man who exercised the horses. At five foot two, we were the same height. He wore his riding clothes, and I assumed he'd just finished with the horses. With one hand, he clutched a heavy saddle I assumed he'd taken off a horse. He stood in front of me, staring at me with his dark eyes.

"Sorry, I didn't mean to bump into you," he said.

"That's okay. I wasn't paying attention to where I was going," I said.

"I overheard you talking to Danielle," he said.

"She was upset that Corbin isn't here. What do you think happened to him?" I asked. "Do you really think he left for good?"

Olson looked around to see if anyone was nearby. Was he going to tell me some big secret?

"I don't know what to think." His voice was a little lower now.

That was it? That wasn't some big secret.

"It's crazy what happened," he said, running his hand through his hair. "I saw you looking around in Mandy's truck."

"Uh-oh," Charlotte said.

I didn't know what to say.

"You can't deny it," Maureen said. "He obviously saw you."

"I thought she was over there, so I was going to talk with her."

He smiled. "Don't worry, I won't tell her. I don't like her anyway. She manipulates people, and she's not good to the animals either."

"That is not true," Ramon said.

"Are you trying to solve this murder?" His fixed stare on my face didn't budge. "Are you a private investigator?"

"I'm just interested in the killer being brought to justice," I said.

Olson looked around again. "I have some information that might be useful."

"Now we're talking," Charlotte said.

"Do tell," Maureen leaned closer.

"What's that?" I asked.

Once again, he scanned the area to see if anyone was watching us. "I saw Mandy around the vet's truck the morning of Ramon's death."

"That doesn't necessarily mean anything," Ramon said. "She works with horses."

"Yes, but she doesn't administer drugs to the horses. That's for the vet to do," Charlotte said.

"Did she take anything from the vet's truck?" I asked.

Olson moved the saddle from one arm to the other. "I'm not sure."

"She looked as if she was suspicious though."

"How so?" I asked.

"She kept looking around to see if anyone was watching her."

"That does sound shady," Charlotte said.

"Did you tell the police about this?"

He shook his head. "I was gone for a while, and I just got back. They haven't contacted me." He looked at the time on his phone. "I'd better go."

"Thanks for the information," I said.

"No problem. I'll let you know if I find out anything else." Olson walked away.

I scanned the area. Maybe I just had an uneasy feeling because of what he'd told me, but it felt as if someone was watching me. It was as if a set of eyes followed my every move. Peering to the right, I spotted a horse looking at me. I laughed. Now I knew who had been spying on me . . . at least I hoped that was who'd been watching.

After clicking off the call, I had somehow managed to get the vet info from Danielle. It had been hard to explain why I wanted that kind of information. It had nothing to do with fashion or Derby hats. Danielle was probably suspicious.

"Good detective work, Cookie," Charlotte said with a wink.

"Thank you," I said as I held my head up high.

I was kind of proud of myself for figuring out all of this. After all, I was completely out of my element here. I was much more at ease back home in my shop. Speaking of which, I missed it a lot. I was beginning to become a little homesick. This was no time for emotions though. I had work to do.

I hopped in the car and drove over to the location. Unfortunately, I got lost on the way there. The ghosts made it even worse by trying to help me find it. I ended up on the expressway and couldn't get off at the right exit because of the traffic.

"Turn here," Charlotte yelled.

I swerved into the right lane and managed to make the turn.

Once I found the correct address, I parked across the street from the brick building. When the traffic eased up, I was able to cross the street. The veterinarian's office was in a brick structure that housed several other businesses.

"It's much busier here than it is in Sugar Creek," Charlotte said. "Though this is nothing compared to a place like New York City."

"That's a big place," I said.

"I often thought of myself as a city girl. I should

have lived there. It's too late now. Or maybe not. Would you consider moving to New York City?" Charlotte asked as she walked along beside me.

"No way," I said.

"What about a visit?"

I walked up the steps of the building. "Maybe a visit."

I stepped inside the building. The woman behind the desk looked up at me when I approached.

"May I help you?"

"I'm here to speak with Dr. Rivere."

Her eyes darkened. "She's not here now."

That was disappointing. I had hoped to talk with her right away.

"Do you know when she will be back?" I asked.

Her expression grew even sadder.

I noticed the room was suspiciously empty. There were no people waiting with their animals. Maybe she was out on calls.

"I don't know when she will be back. She hasn't called to let us know."

"What? That is odd." Maureen and Charlotte stepped closer.

"What do you mean?" I asked.

"She's usually here by now, but she hasn't called, and I'm beginning to become worried."

This was not what I had wanted to hear. After what had happened recently, anytime someone was even a few minutes late, I worried.

"Thank you for the information," I said.

I walked out of the building with the ghosts following.

"Do you think she is missing too?" Charlotte asked.

"I hope not, but it certainly makes me suspicious."

"I wonder if the police know about this?" Maureen asked.

"Probably not," I said as I crossed the street again. "I will tell Dylan and ask his opinion."

From the corner of my eye, I saw a flash of something.

"Cookie, look out!" Charlotte screamed.

Chapter 20

Cookie's Savvy Tips for Vintage Shopping

*Take into consideration the amount of repairs
a garment needs before purchasing it.
Are you willing to make the investment it needs?*

I lunged forward and took a dive against the pavement, just missing the truck.

"Are you okay, Cookie?" Charlotte asked with panic in her voice.

I couldn't speak. Hitting the ground had completely knocked the wind out of me. I was in complete shock at what had just happened. I managed to crawl up from the ground.

"Oh, good, she's not dead," Ramon said.

My dress had a tiny smudge on it, but other than that, I had only a small scrape on my hand. How I had survived was a mystery to me.

"Look at that—not a hair out of place nor makeup smudged," Charlotte said with a smile.

She was trying to make me laugh, but I was

finding it awfully hard. I appreciated her trying to make me feel better though. The black truck had driven off and managed to get away without me being able to get the license plate number or a description of who was driving. No one seemed to even notice what had happened. The other cars zoomed by without as much as a glance my way.

"Did you get a look at the driver?" I asked.

The ghosts shook their heads.

"I think we were just too focused on you," Maureen said. "Plus, the truck sped away so quickly."

"I can tell you one thing," Charlotte said. "This was not an accident."

"That is kind of a given," Ramon said.

"Oh, be quiet," Charlotte said with a wave of her hand.

I marched toward my car, brushing the dirt from my dress as I went. "I'll tell you what is a given. I am going to find out who drives that truck and make sure they go to jail."

"I think that if you find out who is driving that truck, you also will find out who murdered Ramon," Charlotte said.

I opened the car door and slid behind the wheel.

"You think it's the same person?" Ramon asked from the backseat.

"Yes, I do," Charlotte and I said at the same time.

She was in the passenger seat now. Maureen was in the back with Ramon.

"Where are we going?" Charlotte asked as we pulled away from the curb.

"I don't know," I said.

I was angry and confused. Someone had tried to kill me, and I wasn't about to let them get away with it without a fight from me.

"You need to tell Dylan," Maureen said.

Charlotte and I exchanged a look. That was a possibility. It might be what I should have done, but I wasn't completely convinced that I would tell him. He would only worry and not want me to drive anywhere without a police escort. I didn't want him to worry, although it was true that if I told him, he might find out who did this. Even though I wasn't sure what my next move was, I found myself driving toward the bed-and-breakfast. I needed time to regroup and think of a plan. Plus, I needed a change of clothing. I couldn't solve this mystery with a dirty dress, now could I?

Chapter 21

Grandma Pearl's Pearls of Wisdom

*When life hands you lemons,
put a slice in your sweet tea.*

When I stepped into the room, Wind Song was on top of the dresser. That sounded better than saying my grandmother was on top of the dresser. She knocked the tarot cards off with a shove of her delicate paw. They floated down and landed on the floor. Now the cards were scattered about.

"Grandma Pearl, what are you doing?" I asked.

She jumped from the dresser, sailed through the air, and landed on the bed. Grandma Pearl stared down at the cards.

"I think she's trying to tell you something," Charlotte said.

"I suppose she is, but what is the message? Grandma Pearl, what are you trying to tell me?" I asked.

She jumped down onto the floor, sitting in front

of the cards. Next, she pulled out one card by
dragging it away from the others with her paw.
She repeated that two more times until she had
selected three separate cards.

"I guess there's your answer," Charlotte said.

I reached down and picked up the three cards,
although I had no idea what they meant. Heather
had tried to explain each card to me when she'd
given me the deck, but I just couldn't remember. It
was too much detail to take in at one sitting.

"You have to find out what the message is. It
could be important," Charlotte said.

I knew that it was important that we find out.

"What do you mean, Grandma Pearl?"

Wind Song licked her paws. Apparently,
Grandma Pearl was finished talking. I knew
Grandma Pearl enjoyed spending time with me,
but I was pretty sure she didn't enjoy the hair balls.

"Well, you're just going to have to call Heather
and ask her about the cards," Charlotte said.

I placed the cards down and studied them. It was
no use, I couldn't remember anything that Heather
had told me. I should have taken notes. I dialed
Heather, but unfortunately, she didn't answer.

"What will you do now?" Ramon asked as he
paced across the bedroom floor.

His movements were silent across the large
Oriental rug that lay in the middle of the floor.

"I know what you can do." Maureen held up her
index finger as if she'd had a eureka moment.

"What's that?" Charlotte and I asked in unison.

"You can ask the guy at the occult shop."

"That's a good idea." Ramon stopped pacing.

"Well, get your purse, Cookie. We're going for a ride." Charlotte hurried over to the door.

Within a couple of minutes, we'd slipped out of the bed-and-breakfast and were now headed toward the occult shop.

"I hope he knows what he's talking about," Charlotte said. "He looks awfully young."

"Well, I also left a message for Heather. I'm sure she'll call me back. In the meantime, we can try this guy."

We pulled up to the shop. Traffic had died down, and there were no people walking along the sidewalk.

"Why is it so quiet?" I asked as we walked along.

"Well, this is a high-crime area," Ramon said. "So most people don't walk around here after dark."

"And you're just now telling me this?" I hurried my steps as we approached the shop's entrance.

The hours listed on the window said the shop closed in thirty minutes. When I stepped inside the shop, I didn't see the guy we'd met before. I hoped that he was working. I probably wouldn't ask anyone else. He seemed friendly, like he would want to help.

"You're back with the ghosts."

I spun around.

"Why does he keep popping up like that?" Charlotte asked with her hand on her heart.

"What brings you by this late?" He tossed the bangs out of his eyes.

I hoped he didn't think I was weird for what I was about to ask. I pulled the cards out from my purse. "I wondered if you could tell me what these mean."

He took the cards. "Uh-huh." He looked at the first card. "Uh-huh." He studied the second card. "Uh-huh." Then the third.

"For heaven's sake," Charlotte said. "Just tell her what they mean."

He held up one of the cards. "This card is for friendship."

"Oh? Well, that's not bad."

"Yes, but this card." He held up one that depicted a monster. It has horns and a devil.

"This is evil," he said.

Maureen swayed a little as if she might faint. "Oh, Cookie, throw the cards away."

"Getting rid of the cards won't make what they mean go away," Ramon said.

"The cards are connected. The last one means beware."

"Beware of evil? That could mean a lot of things." Charlotte paced around the guy.

He looked to his left as if he'd heard what Charlotte said.

"You brought the ghosts with you again?"

"You sense them?" I asked.

He looked around again as if he was trying to locate the spirits. "Yes, I guess you do too."

I chuckled. "They're with me all the time."

He frowned. "That's not good."

Whether it was good or not was neither here nor there. The ghosts were not going anywhere anytime soon.

"The message from the cards means beware of the friend. Something evil has a hold of the friendship." He handed the cards back.

"What friendship?" I asked.

"That's something you will have to figure out. Why do you have the cards if you can't read them?" he asked.

"You should tell him the truth, Cookie. He obviously has some psychic ability," Charlotte said.

I cleared my throat. "Okay, here goes. I asked about the cards because my cat told me to ask."

All right, that didn't sound so great. And there was no way I was ready to tell anyone else the truth. He quirked an eyebrow. He was probably seconds away from calling the police to have me escorted out.

"I meant to say my grandmother. She told me."

That was technically the truth. He had looked at me like I was crazy when I'd said my cat told me to ask.

"Well, I guess that's close enough," Charlotte said.

I thanked him for helping me and headed back to the bed-and-breakfast. Nothing else could be done that night.

Chapter 22

Cookie's Savvy Tips for Vintage Shopping

*Don't be afraid to venture out of your comfort zone.
Just because it's not something you'd usually wear
doesn't mean you can't wear it.*

All of a sudden, a loud scream rang through the bed-and-breakfast, echoing off the walls. I practically jumped off the bed. Maureen and Charlotte jumped.

"Oh, for heaven's sake. What is going on in this place? It's worse than a haunted house. I've seen less scary things at the movies," Charlotte said.

"If I wasn't dead, that would have scared me to death." Maureen fanned herself.

I jumped up and rushed over to the door of my room. Hannah had screamed, but I had no idea why.

"Let's just hope that she saw a mouse or something, and nothing worse," I said as I hurried toward the door.

"A mouse is bad," Charlotte said.

I rushed out the door and down the stairs, trying not to fall and tumble to the bottom. When I reached the foyer, I made a left into the living room and found Hannah standing in the middle of the room, as if she'd seen a ghost.

The ghosts had been with me up in my room, so I knew it wasn't one of them. Had another ghost appeared? I certainly hoped not.

"Hannah, what's wrong?" I asked as I ran over to her.

"She looks as if she might faint," Maureen said.

"Get some water and splash it on her," Charlotte said.

I knew that Charlotte would like nothing more than for me to do that, but I wasn't quite sure that was necessary just yet.

"I just saw someone peeking in the window," Hannah said.

I looked over her shoulder at the window behind her. "Which window?"

The room had four windows—two on the front of the house and two on the side. The other walls were entrances to the kitchen and the foyer.

"It was that window right over there," Hannah said, pointing to the window behind her, which was at the front of the house.

I ran over to see if someone was still standing there.

"Don't go over there. They might see you," she said.

They had already seen her, so what difference

did it make if they saw me? I wanted to actually catch someone looking in the window. What did they think they were doing? That was just creepy. Something rattled.

"What was that?"

I didn't want to tell her that it sounded like a doorknob rattling. I had to be brave.

I peered out the window at the trees, the surrounding flowers, and the shrubs, but there was no sign of a person.

"Hannah, are you sure there was someone out here?"

She nodded. "Yes." Her words were barely audible.

This must really have scared her a lot if she was too scared to speak.

"I'm absolutely sure someone was looking in the window. I think they were trying to break in—probably to kill us," she said.

"That's a terrible thing to say," Charlotte said.

"Let's not jump to any conclusions. Maybe it was someone looking for a room," I said.

"I'm not letting anyone that creepy stay here. Look around."

I moved over to the other window to take a look, but it was the same thing. There was no sign of a person.

"Wait right here, Hannah, I'm going to go outside and take a look around."

"Are you sure that's such a good idea?" Charlotte asked. "You don't want to be the one murdered."

Everyone was jumping to conclusions. We needed to stay calm. Just because someone had recently been murdered didn't mean that it would happen again, nor that it would happen here at the bed-and-breakfast.

"I'll go with you, Cookie," Ramon said.

I moved to the dining room and then into the kitchen. The old screen door squeaked and banged shut behind me as I went out the back door. I'd meant to be quiet on my way out, but the door had slipped out of my hand. I froze, wondering if the person who had been out here had heard the noise. There was no sign of anyone, so I went around to the side of the house.

Still nothing seemed unusual. I walked close to the window and peeked in. Hannah was standing almost in the same spot, looking terrified. She was waiting for me to return. I hoped she wouldn't look over and see me at the window. It would scare her all over again, thinking that I was the person she'd seen before.

I noticed that some of the flowers looked as if they'd been stepped on. Hannah was right: someone had been there. I noticed a footprint to the right. Just one, which was odd.

I backed away from the window so that I could turn around and go back into the house—and bumped right into someone. I let out another scream, but when I turned around, I realized that Ken was the one standing behind me. He grabbed my arms to keep me from falling.

"Cookie, are you all right? I'm sorry if I scared you."

I managed to catch my breath, although my heart was still pounding pretty fast. "I'm fine. I just didn't know you were behind me."

"Exactly why are you looking in the window?" Ken asked.

"Hannah thought she saw someone peeking in, so I came out here to take a look."

"Really? Maybe I should take a look around," he said.

"I haven't seen anyone so far. I did notice the footprint in the dirt right here."

Ken looked down. "Are you sure it didn't come from your shoe?"

"It looks small, but it's not mine," I said.

Without warning, a drizzle of rain fell.

Ken touched my arm. "Come on. We'll go back inside. I don't want you to get wet."

Hannah insisted we have a cup of tea with her. She said it would calm our nerves. Ken had checked again for any sign of someone wandering around outside, but the person was never seen again. The size of the shoe print made me think it was possibly a woman, though Hannah thought it was a man.

Chapter 23

Grandma Pearl's Pearls of Wisdom

You don't have to be hateful.
Just say, "Bless your heart."

The sun had just peeked over the horizon. Soon I would have to get ready for the big day ahead.

It seemed like the best place to find any information was at the barn. I decided to go there and see if anyone else had information for me. It certainly wouldn't hurt to ask. Soon the Derby would be over, and everyone would be gone. It would be almost impossible to solve the murder after that. If I didn't do it now, it would forever be a cold case. Unless, of course, the police had clues that I wasn't aware of, but I thought I'd done a fairly good job of finding things. Dylan was working on getting more information at this exact minute.

The barn was quiet, except for the sounds of the horses. It was mid-morning, and things had settled down after all the horses had been fed and exercised. I didn't see Danielle, Mandy, or anyone I knew. The ghosts were quietly following behind me. It was unusual for them not to be chatting away, but I was enjoying the break. I shuffled along the dirt path over to the office area, thinking I might find someone there. Twisting the knob, I realized the door was locked. I headed back over toward the stalls. If I didn't see anyone this time, I would leave. I'd made it halfway across the lot when I spotted something on the ground.

"Look, it's a phone," Charlotte said at the same moment.

I reached down and picked it up. I looked around to see who might have dropped it. There were a few people at other barns, but they all looked occupied and as though they couldn't have been over here anytime recently.

"See if it turns on so you can see who owns it," Charlotte said.

After scanning my surroundings one more time, I swiped the screen. To my surprise, the phone was still working.

"It still has a charge," I said happily.

"Good. Now find out who it belongs to," Maureen said.

When I looked up the owner's info, I was shocked to find out who it belonged to.

"This phone belongs to Mandy," I said.

Charlotte's eyes widened. "Check out everything on it."

"You'd better take it back to your car just in case she comes back looking for it," Ramon said.

"He has a good point," Charlotte said.

I slipped the phone into my pocket and hurried back toward my car. I couldn't wait to see what I could find on the phone. Maybe it would be nothing though. I got in the car and hurriedly swiped the phone back on.

There wasn't much battery life left, so I needed to hurry. I didn't even know which part to look at first. I decided to look in the notes section. There were just more poems written there.

"She really loves those awful poems," Charlotte said.

I looked through the contacts but didn't see anything unusual.

"Check the photos," Maureen said.

I went to the photos and scrolled through. That was when I saw the photo of Mandy and Danielle. It must have been taken in happier times because they were actually smiling. Well, halfhearted smiles, but that was still something. I studied the photo for a long moment. That was when I noticed something on Danielle's wrist.

"What is that?" I asked.

"What is what?" Charlotte asked.

The ghosts leaned in for a closer look. I zoomed in on the screen. Danielle was wearing a bracelet. But it wasn't just any bracelet. It was exactly like the one that had been found at the crime scene.

"I see what you're talking about," Charlotte said.

"What is it?" Maureen and Ramon asked in unison.

"It couldn't be, could it? Danielle wouldn't do something like this."

"Anything is possible," Charlotte said.

"Tell us," Maureen said.

"The bracelet that Danielle is wearing is just like the one that was found at the scene."

"Do you think Danielle killed me?" Ramon asked.

"I don't know . . . I didn't think she would be capable of such a thing," I said, still staring at the photo.

"We need to ask her about the bracelet," Charlotte said.

How could I ask any questions with ghosts talking in my ear? Nevertheless, Charlotte was right yet again. I needed to ask Danielle. If she'd lost her bracelet, I would know that she was the killer. Or at least it would be reasonable to think that. But she would be suspicious that I was on to her if I asked. I would have to think of a clever way to find out if she'd lost the bracelet. In the meantime, I didn't know what to do with the phone.

"What do I do with this thing?" I asked.

"You have to keep it," Charlotte said.

"What if the police need to see it?" I asked.

"You can't let anyone have it right now." Charlotte reached for the phone, but, of course, she didn't make contact.

I was so confused and didn't know what I should do. It would be easy to turn the phone in to the police. Maybe they would really appreciate a look at it. I stuffed it into my pocket though I was still torn about what to do.

"Oh no," Charlotte said.

"What is it?" I asked.

"Mandy is here. It looks as if she is looking for something too."

I followed Charlotte's pointing finger and spotted Mandy. She was looking on the ground and at the same time headed this way. It definitely looked as if she was searching for something. I was frozen to the spot. She would probably know that I had the phone if she spotted me. I would have *guilty* written all over my face. Maybe I should just toss it back onto the ground and run away.

"If she sees you with it, she will probably freak out."

"Maybe I should leave it where I found it," I said.

Charlotte shook her head. "It's too late now. She's looking this way."

"I don't want to talk with her right now." I hurried away from the area.

I was hoping Mandy wouldn't come after me. I glanced over my shoulder every few seconds to see if she was following me. I got the impression that she was suspicious of me. Of course, I locked the car door and prepared to start the engine immediately so I could get out of there.

I had my hand on the key in the ignition when a knock sounded on the window. I couldn't hold back my scream as I jumped. The ghosts screamed too. Mandy was standing by the window.

"Drive away," Maureen said.

It was as if the boogeyman had jumped out from under the bed and found me. Everyone in the car was panicked. Mandy stared at me with a confused expression. She probably wondered why I wasn't lowering the window. I guess I had no choice but to talk to her. It would be too awkward to take Maureen's suggestion and drive away.

"Just act casual and calm," Charlotte said as I rolled down the window.

I forced a smile even though I was panicked. "Hi, Mandy. How's it going?"

She stared at me for a second. "I've lost my phone. You didn't happen to see it when you were walking around, did you?"

Now would be the real test. Could I pull off the lie adequately? My heart thumped faster.

"No, I didn't see a phone. Sorry."

I felt bad about lying. But I couldn't give the phone back now, could I?

She watched my face. "I can't find it anywhere."

"Sorry I couldn't help more."

She looked around.

"Drive away," Maureen said again.

I couldn't take off with her still standing by the car door. But what did she want? I told her I hadn't seen the phone. Was she suspicious? She had to be. That was why she was still there by the car. She probably saw me looking at something. The phone was in my pocket. If she knew it was right there, no doubt she would have freaked out.

"Would you mind giving me a ride?" Mandy asked.

"Say no," Charlotte said. "She is up to something, Cookie. You have to tell her no."

I was never good at telling people no. "Sure, I guess I could do that."

"No!" The ghosts said in unison.

Even Ramon didn't want me to give her a ride.

"Great. Thanks," Mandy said as she moved around to the other side of the car.

"What are you thinking, Cookie? What if she is the killer? What if she sees the phone in your pocket?"

"She can't see through fabric," I said. "You'll have to move to the backseat, Charlotte."

"Oh, great. You give her a ride, and I have to go to the backseat. You know I get carsick back there. This just keeps getting worse."

Mandy opened the car door and slid in. "I really like your car."

"Thanks," I said as I cranked the ignition.

An awkward silence fell over us. I was more than a little tense. I wished I had been able to tell her no. I hadn't thought of an excuse fast enough though.

"So where do you need to go?" I asked as I backed out of the parking space.

"I just need to go to the store around the corner," Mandy said with a smile.

Her smile didn't seem genuine though. I wasn't sure what it was about her, but she gave off a creepy vibe—dare I say almost an evil one? I was surprised that the horses didn't pick up on her strange vibe. I didn't consider myself sensitive to other people, but she was putting out strong feelings. I pulled into the street and headed for the store. I had to admit I was speeding a little because I wanted to get her out of my car. She was quiet for most of the trip.

"I really need to find that phone. I hope no one picked it up and decided to keep it. I would hate to see what happened to them if I find that out."

I pulled into the parking lot. I stared at her somewhat in disbelief at what she'd just said.

"That is creepy," Charlotte said.

"She is strange," Maureen said.

Ramon was quiet. I think there was something he wasn't sharing with me about Mandy. Mandy opened the car door and stared at me, which made me completely uncomfortable.

"Thanks again," she said with that fake smile.

As soon as she closed the door, Charlotte said, "Now get out of here before she gets back in the car."

I punched the gas and pulled out of the parking lot. Now that Mandy was out of the car, the air had lightened. But I still was spooked from the whole experience.

"Ramon, is there something you are forgetting to tell me about Mandy?" I asked.

"He forgot to mention how completely weird she is," Charlotte said.

"Not that I can remember," Ramon said quietly.

"Tell the truth." Charlotte was back in the front seat.

"I am telling the truth," Ramon said.

When I checked the rearview mirror, Ramon was looking out the window. It looked as if there was something on his mind. Maybe it was just the fact that he was stuck in this situation. I stopped at a red light.

"Hey, what is that?" Charlotte pointed at the seat beside her.

I reached down and picked up a piece of paper. I was sure it wasn't mine.

I opened up the folded paper. "It's a poem."

Charlotte and I exchanged a look. I knew right away who this belonged to.

"What does it say?" Charlotte asked.

Maureen leaned forward in the backseat. Ramon remained in his spot, but he was looking at me. There seemed to be fear in his eyes.

"Bad things happen to those who lie," I read it out.

"What? Is that what it says?" Ramon leaned forward in the seat now.

Why was he freaking out? I knew he wasn't telling me everything. Why did she leave this unless it was some kind of threat?

"You should tell the police about this," Maureen said.

"I can, but I have a feeling she will just deny it. That seems to be her way. She has that innocent act down pat."

Chapter 24

Cookie's Savvy Tips for Vintage Shopping

❦

Don't be afraid to negotiate.
It's okay to ask for a lower price.

As I drove farther away from the track, Dylan called.

"Can you meet me?" he asked.

The tone of his voice made it sound as if this was something a bit serious.

"Sure. Is everything okay?" I asked.

"Yes, just a few things to tell you that I just found out."

Now I was really curious. It sounded like this was good info.

"I'll meet you at the same restaurant," I said.

"See you soon," Dylan said.

"What did he say?" Charlotte asked.

"He has some information for me. I guess it's about the case."

"I'm really excited," Charlotte said. "Where are we meeting him?"

"At the same restaurant," I said.

"Well, that would not be my first choice, but nevertheless, punch it." Charlotte motioned toward the road.

When I reached the restaurant, I parked next to Dylan's car. Once inside, I scanned the place for him. Dylan was already sitting at a table in the corner. He waved for me to come on over. The place was more crowded this time.

Dylan pulled the chair out for me, and I sat down. "You look lovely," he said.

"Doesn't she though?" Charlotte ran her hand through Dylan's hair.

He frowned and felt the air above him. "Must be a draft in here."

"Thank you," I said.

When he looked away, I gave Charlotte a warning glare. The waitress came over and brought me a menu and a glass of water.

"Tell her to just go away. You want to know what he has to say." Charlotte stepped close to the waitress.

She had very little patience.

When the waitress walked away, I said, "So tell me what you found out."

Okay, so I had very little patience as well.

"You get right to the point, don't you?" Dylan said with a smile.

"There's little time to waste," I said, also with a smile.

"Well, they took Kristina in for questioning."

I immediately looked at Ramon. Of course, he was upset. I hated to see him like this, hated for him to think that his wife had murdered him.

"What? Don't be so surprised," Charlotte said. "You were cheating on her."

That was hardly a reason to murder someone though. I wanted to tell Ramon that everything would be okay, but I knew that wasn't the case.

"Is something wrong?" Dylan asked.

He had noticed that I was distracted. He looked over his shoulder to see what I was looking at. I forced myself to look away from the ghosts.

"What was their reason for taking her in?" I asked.

"Well, he was having an affair."

"Ha. We already knew that," Charlotte said, as if we'd just scored the first point in the game.

"Cookie is savvier than the police," Maureen said.

I didn't know about that. I'd gotten lucky.

"I'm glad that you found this information, but I wonder what will happen to her next."

"She'll probably go to prison," Charlotte said.

"I guess they'll arrest her. We'll find out more information later today."

"Keep me posted," I said.

"Absolutely. So are we going shopping for my Derby outfit?"

"Of course," I said, grabbing my bag. "I just

need to go back to the bed-and-breakfast for a quick change."

"Sure. I can meet you at the vintage shop," Dylan said.

"Actually, it's kind of out of the way."

"He's going to get suspicious eventually," Charlotte said.

Dylan stared for a moment. "All right. I'll see you soon."

We didn't know that he would be suspicious. As long as I had a good excuse, maybe he wouldn't be. After saying good-bye to Dylan, I left the restaurant and headed for the bed-and-breakfast. Ken was probably wondering where I was. I pulled up to the house and hurried to the door.

As soon as I walked inside, I saw Ken in the hallway.

"I'm glad you're back," he said.

"Is something wrong?" I asked.

"I have something to show you. Come over here. I can put it on the television."

What in the world could he possibly have to show me? When he put on the screen, Mandy's face appeared. She was talking to the reporters. They did a whole segment talking about the race tomorrow, interviewing her.

"What's so wrong about that?" Ramon asked.

The way that she talked was really weird. It was almost as if she was saying right there on TV that she was glad Ramon was gone.

Ramon tossed his hands up. "Why is everyone so glad that I'm gone? Was I really that bad of a person, or do I seem bad now?"

"You're not too bad, I suppose, but maybe you were different when you were alive." Charlotte studied her bright red fingernails.

"Yeah, you were probably a real jerk," Maureen said.

Mandy was definitely acting weird. During the interview, she talked fast and fidgeted. Plus she had a nervous laugh. Maybe it was just because she knew she was on TV.

"You seem a little bit stressed," Ken said when he turned off the television.

"I guess all of this is kind of stressing me out, to be honest. I'll be glad when we're back in Sugar Creek." I rubbed my arms as if fighting off a chill. Seeing Mandy on TV still had me creeped out.

"Well, it's almost finished now. Keep your chin up." Ken touched my chin with his index finger. "So are you going to help me pick out that outfit?"

"You agreed to pick out an outfit for him too?" Charlotte said. "Oh, what a tangled web we weave."

I'd never lied to Ken or Dylan. Maybe just withheld information.

"You're going to have to do something," Maureen said.

"Sure, we can arrange something. How about later today?" I asked.

"What about solving the murders? There's no time for shopping," Ramon said.

I would just squeeze the shopping in somehow.

"Later is fine. Do you have plans now?"

"Actually, yes. I was just checking on Wind Song." I gestured toward upstairs.

Ken touched my arm. "Sure, we can talk later."

I left Ken downstairs as I hurried up to my room to change and check on Wind Song again. It felt strange to walk into the room and see my grandmother eating Tuna Delight. I had to remember the cat was in there too. I slipped into a cute 1970s blue cotton sleeveless dress. It had a pointed collar and a bodice that buttoned all the way down the front. After putting on my white leather sandals with a white flower bloom attached to the top of each, I headed back out the door.

"Wind Song is really becoming accustomed to this house and seems to be feeling right at home," Charlotte said.

"Well, this house does look like my grandmother's old place."

I hurried out the door before Ken could stop me again. I wouldn't be able to fib for much longer.

As we drove to meet Dylan, Charlotte said, "You know, you have to tell Dylan that Ken is here. You really can't hide it any longer. They will see each other at the Derby."

I sighed. "I guess you're right."

It was just easier to avoid the situation. I couldn't keep doing that though. Eventually I had to face the truth. Charlotte was right. I had to tell Dylan.

Dylan's car was parked in the lot when I arrived at the vintage shop. As I parked the Buick, he got out of his car.

"I was getting worried about you." He leaned down and kissed me.

"There was a lot of traffic."

"Well, you're here now. Help me find the right outfit." He took my hand, and we walked to the door.

"You have a great sense of style," I said.

Dylan opened the shop door for me. "I'd hate to see what I picked out on my own."

The shop was just as jam-packed full of clothing as the first time I'd visited. Maybe I should have tried a different store. Luckily, I spotted the overhead sign for men's clothing at the back of the store.

"I think he's just trying to make you feel better," Maureen said.

"We should start with pants," I said, motioning for Dylan to follow me.

"Pants would be good. He'd get strange looks without them." Charlotte laughed.

I picked several options for Dylan to try. "Here you are. Try these."

I stood outside the dressing room with the ghosts.

"I hate shopping," Ramon said, leaning against the wall.

While Dylan was dressing, I figured I would casually mention the fact that Ken was in town and staying in the bed-and-breakfast. I should have told Dylan a long time ago.

"What do you think?" Dylan asked, showing me the first pick.

He turned around, giving me a full view of the outfit. His 1940s twill pants had cuffed leg openings and two side pockets, as well as two welt pockets on the back. The cotton shirt was also from the forties. The brown collar and sleeves paired well with the yellow body of the shirt. It had two front flap pockets and a single pleat in the back. The forties was my favorite decade for clothing. I loved the utilitarian look of the styles.

"I think it's good, but you should try the others too."

He smiled. "I thought you might say that."

Dylan stepped back into the dressing room.

"There is something I need to tell you," I said.

Charlotte wagged her finger. "Oh sure, wait until he can't see your face."

"What's that?" Dylan asked.

"It's about Ken. You remember him."

Dylan peeked out the door with a frown on his face. "Yes, I know him. I get the feeling I'm not going to like what you're about to say."

"You got that right, man," Ramon said.

"I should have told you this sooner," I said.

I looked around and noticed that Charlotte was up to something. That was when I saw the mannequin slowly move. She was going to try to knock that thing over. Why, I wasn't quite sure. I made a dash across the room, almost knocking over racks of clothing, just to keep the mannequin from falling.

At least my mad dash across the room was better than someone thinking that the place was haunted. If the mannequin fell over without anyone touching it, they'd think it was a ghost. I managed to reach the mannequin, and I even got a hold of it for a second, but before my hand had a good grip, it completely fell to the floor. Unfortunately, I also was unable to keep myself from going down with it. I landed with a loud crash on the floor on top of the mannequin. The ghosts seemed to find this extremely humorous. They were laughing loudly.

"Oh, you look really cool, Cookie," Charlotte said.

Yeah, I knew. Thanks to her. She was the one who started this.

"Cookie, are you all right?" Dylan asked.

He hurried over and managed to help me up from the floor. I wiped off my clothing and straightened it.

"Yes, I'm fine," I said.

I would talk to the ghosts later about this. "I just wanted to look at a blouse that was on the mannequin, and I accidentally knocked it over."

"Wow, you must have been in a hurry to look at it. You made a dash for that thing," Dylan said.

"Sometimes I get excited about vintage clothing," I said.

"Clearly," he said with a smile.

Of course, the ghosts were still laughing. I didn't think it was all that funny. Okay, maybe it was a little funny, but one thing had happened. I guessed that that was Charlotte's plan all along. Dylan and I were laughing, and he seemed to have forgotten all about the thing with Ken. Yes, that was Charlotte's plan. She'd figured out a way to make things happy again. She might be a little rough around the edges, but she really was a good friend.

Chapter 25

Grandma Pearl's Pearls of Wisdom

It's a serious problem if sweet tea can't fix it.

"Well, Dylan really knows how to work around things and get things going his way," Charlotte said.

She was saying this because Dylan and I were picking out clothing for Ken. Dylan said there was no reason to make two trips since we were already there. I knew he was just trying to keep me from going anywhere with Ken. It had worked because I didn't have the heart to disagree with him. We'd picked up gray cotton pants and a blue and gray short-sleeved cotton shirt.

Saying good-bye to Dylan, we agreed to meet later. I headed back to the bed-and-breakfast. Now I had to explain to Ken that I had bought his outfit without him. After all, he had asked me to buy it for him.

"I'm still impressed by how Dylan handled the situation," Ramon said from the backseat.

"He is smooth," Maureen said.

"I told Cookie that from the beginning," Charlotte said.

I didn't comment as I continued to navigate the road. I pulled into the driveway. Ken's car wasn't there.

"Well, at least now you have a bit of time before you have to explain that outfit to him," Charlotte said.

"Actually, I'd rather do it now."

I had worked up what I was going to say. Regardless, I grabbed his clothing and headed inside. When I stepped inside, everything was quiet. I had expected to see Hannah. The only sound was the ticking of the old grandfather clock in the hallway.

I headed up the stairs to my room. At the top of the stairs, I paused. There was a single brown loafer—only one shoe—and it appeared to be Hannah's. I'd seen her wearing this pair earlier. This was odd. I picked up the shoe and called out for Hannah. A creepy feeling settled in my stomach. Hannah didn't answer when I called for her.

"Cookie, I'm getting a strange vibe," Charlotte said.

"Me too," I whispered.

"You should be careful," Maureen said.

I left the outfit in my room and decided to look

for Hannah. I went over to her room. The door was open. I'd noticed during my stay that it had always been closed. I stepped just beyond the threshold and called out her name again. I didn't want to invade her private space. An iron bed with a baby blue bedspread sat centered in the room against the wall. The walls were covered with a golden striped wallpaper. Antique chairs and a table were placed in front of the window that overlooked the backyard.

"It doesn't look as if she's here," Charlotte said, walking completely into the room.

Charlotte and the other ghosts didn't have the same concern for private space as they stood in the middle of the room. Something felt wrong. When Hannah didn't answer, I stepped further into the room.

"I don't think she's here," I said.

"You should look in the closet," Charlotte said.

"Why would she be in the closet?" I asked.

Charlotte walked over and stuck her head through the door. "Nope, not there."

I took a peek under the bed. I didn't know why, but it seemed like the only other place someone could hide. Was this a game of hide and seek? I got a bad vibe from this.

A noise sounded from somewhere in the house. I stopped.

"Did you hear that?" I whispered.

The ghosts nodded.

"I heard it. Sounded like it came from out in the hallway," Ramon said.

When I stepped out into the hallway, the noise sounded again.

"It sounds like it's coming from above," Charlotte said.

"The only thing above is the attic," I said.

"Maybe it's a mouse," Maureen said.

"That's one heck of a mouse," Charlotte said.

That was exactly my thought. If a mouse was big enough to make that kind of noise, then I didn't want to run into it. The loud bang sounded again.

"I think that might be Hannah. Maybe she's trying to get your attention," Charlotte said.

"She could be hurt," Maureen said. "You should go check."

I hated the thought of going up into the attic, but if she needed help, I had to do just that. I went over to the opening for the attic and pulled the lever. The stairs came down, and I released a deep breath. I forced myself to climb up the stairs.

The space was dim, but I could still make out everything. That was when I saw her over in the corner of the room. She was bound up with rope and had a piece of tape over her mouth. Her brow was furrowed, and she shook back and forth. Her words were muffled. I suspected she was saying something, like "Get these ropes off me now!"

"Oh my heavens," Charlotte said.

"Oh my goodness." I raced over to her. "Are you okay?"

"Does she look okay to you?" Charlotte asked.

Of course not, but I had to ask if she had some sort of serious injury. I wiggled the rope, trying to get it undone. Whoever did this had done a really good job. After a struggle, I got her hands loose. Next Hannah and I worked on untying her legs. Once her legs were unbound, she took hold of the edge of the tape, and I grimaced as she ripped it from her mouth.

Now I asked again, "Are you all right?"

"No, I am not all right."

"To be fair, that was a silly question," Charlotte said.

"I was tied up in my attic. I thought I was going to die, so no, I am not all right," she stood up from the floor.

"What happened? How did you get up here?" I asked.

"A couple of men came by and did this to me. They were looking for you," she said as she glared at me.

"For me?" I asked.

"You heard me," she said.

"Oh, this is not good, Cookie," Charlotte said.

"What did they look like? What did they say?" I asked.

I couldn't believe this had happened.

"They were tall, muscular, and mean-looking. That's all I know," she said. "They didn't tell me why they did this. They just asked for you, and when they searched the house and couldn't find you, they stuck me in the attic. They left me to die."

Footsteps sounded from the floor below us.

"Do you think they're back?" Charlotte asked.

I motioned for Hannah not to make a move. I put my finger up to my mouth so that she would remember to be quiet. We had to sneak over to the door and peek. I wanted to find out who was down there. Unfortunately, the old floorboards up there squeaked and moaned with every step. I managed to sneak over to the door. My heart thumped wildly I lifted the door and peeked out. That was when I saw Ken. His back was facing me.

Apparently, he was looking for us. I walked down the stairs. Ken turned around. "Oh, there you are," he said. "What are you doing up there? Trying on more clothing?"

"You won't believe me when I tell you," I whispered.

Hannah was right behind me, coming down the ladder. She was extremely angry, I could tell.

She motioned for me to back off. "I want you out of here." She pointed to Ken. "And him too."

Ken's eyes widened. "What happened? What's going on here?"

"I found her in the attic. She was tied up. Somebody apparently came here looking for me, and that's what they did to her."

"Who were they?" Ken asked.

"That's what we can't figure out. They didn't tell her who they were or why they wanted me, but we're assuming they will be back."

Maybe it was best that I did leave. They would probably be back, looking for me.

"I'll pack my things," I said.

After gathering our things, Ken and I hurried out the door. He carried Wind Song in her carrier.

"This is a shocking turn of events," Charlotte said.

Ken set Wind Song on the front seat of my car. After that, he placed his bags in his car and came back over to mine.

"Where are you going now?" Ken asked.

"I'm not sure," I said.

"You could probably stay with Dylan," Maureen said.

"Good thinking," Charlotte responded.

"I'll probably tell Danielle what happened. Maybe she knows where I can stay for the next two days." Now more than ever, I couldn't wait to get home. "What about you?" I asked.

Ken ran his hand through his hair. "I suppose I could stay in my car."

"I can't let you do that," I said. "Let me make a call."

Most importantly, I had to find out who the men were and why they were looking for me. That was scary. Hannah was still watching us from the window. She'd probably call the police soon if we didn't get out of there. Maybe she already had called. I explained to Danielle what had happened. She wanted me to call the police right away. I'd probably tell Dylan first.

"Good news," I said when I hung up the call.

"What's that?" Ken asked.

"Danielle actually has a couple of extra rooms at the hotel where they're staying. She paid for them, but the people who were coming didn't show up. Looks like they're ours if we want them."

"Dylan isn't going to like this. He will want you to stay with him instead of following Ken," Charlotte said.

I wasn't sure if I was ready to spend that much time with Dylan. We'd only started dating. I wanted to take things slow. I'd go with Ken to the hotel and take it from there. Once again, I'd kept this information from Dylan. It wasn't like I was staying in the same room with Ken. Just the same hotel.

Chapter 26

Cookie's Savvy Tips for Vintage Shopping

*Take a list of items you're looking for.
That way, you'll avoid purchasing
something you might regret.*

Later that night, I had settled into my new hotel room. I'd had to sneak the cat in so the management wouldn't see her. Things had been so hectic that I hadn't gotten a chance to talk with Wind Song about using the Ouija board. I was a bit nervous because I didn't have Heather here to help me this time.

"Grandma, would you like to use the Ouija board?" I asked.

"I'll never get used to you calling the cat 'grandma'," Charlotte said.

"Well, it feels kind of strange not to call her that, knowing she's my grandmother," I said.

"That is the weirdest thing I've ever seen," Ramon said.

"Stranger than the fact that you're a ghost?" I asked.

"Well, I guess there is that," Ramon said.

I pulled out the Ouija board from my luggage and placed it in the middle of the bed. As soon as I sat down on the bed, Wind Song jumped up and sat next to the board.

"I guess she's ready," Charlotte said.

Wind Song placed her paws on the planchette.

"Do you have any clues for Ramon's murder?" I asked.

We watched as Wind Song pushed the planchette across the board.

"What is she saying?" Ramon asked.

She first stopped on the letter R. By the time she had finished, she'd spelled the word *remember*.

"What do you remember, Grandma?" I asked.

Wind Song stared at the board for a moment, as if she was trying to recall. She moved her paw again, starting with the letter M. This time, she spelled out the name *Maureen*.

"What about me?" Maureen asked.

"Do you remember Maureen?" I asked.

Grandma took the planchette over to the word *Yes*.

"She remembers you," I said, looking at Maureen. "Do you remember my grandmother, Pearl Chanel?"

Maureen stared at the cat for a moment. "I remember now. I never knew her last name. She came to the community center. She always wore a hat and gloves."

"Yes, that's her."

"She was such a sweet lady."

"Thank you," I said. "Yes, she is a wonderful woman."

"Does she have anything else to say?" Maureen asked.

"Is there something you can tell us about Maureen?"

Wind Song moved the planchette again. *Affair* was the word she spelled this time.

"Affair?" Maureen and Charlotte said at the same time. "The only cheater we know is Ramon."

They smirked at him.

"Are you ever going to let me forget that?" he asked.

"No," they said.

"Okay, y'all, enough of that. Let's get back to the board. Grandma, tell me what you're talking about. Who is having an affair?"

I assumed she meant Ramon. Was she talking about Ramon's affair? We already knew about that one. We watched with anticipation as Wind Song moved the planchette again. I was excited to see what she had to say this time.

"I can't stand this. Why does it take so long?" Charlotte asked.

"Well, she does have tiny paws. Plus, her range of motion isn't all that great," I said.

Charlotte paced across the room. She'd moved the planchette, with her kitty paws, around to all the different letters. The first word was *Maureen* again. The second word I hadn't expected. She'd spelled out the word *husband*. Charlotte and I exchanged a look. I was pretty sure I knew what my grandmother was trying to say, but I wanted to be positive. I looked at Maureen. She was staring in shock.

"Was Maureen's husband having an affair?" I asked, still watching Maureen.

Wind Song pushed the planchette over to the word *Yes*.

"Oh dear," Charlotte said.

"This isn't good," Ramon said.

He was probably upset because he knew he'd take more heat for his affair now.

Maureen shook her head. "That is simply not possible. I don't know why she would say such a thing."

Maureen paced across the floor, waving her arms. She was clearly upset.

"She's in denial," Charlotte whispered.

"Why do you say this, Grandma? Does it have something to do with Maureen's murder?" I asked.

The kitty paw moved to the word *Yes* again. I bet the person he was having an affair with was the one who killed Maureen.

Maureen was holding her hands up to her ears. I knew she could still hear us though. I had to press on and ask more questions, even if Maureen didn't want to hear.

"Do you know who he was having an affair with?" I asked.

My grandmother moved the planchette over to the word *No*.

"Ugh," Charlotte said. "That figures."

"How does she know he was having an affair?" Maureen asked.

Wind Song jumped down from the bed. She was finished talking with us for now. I'd have to call my mom and Heather to see if they could find out more about this new revelation.

"It's okay, Maureen, try not to worry too much," I said.

"I can't believe that rat was cheating on me. I should have known. He was always sneaky." Maureen clenched her fists.

"She's moved from denial to anger," Ramon said. "This part is not good."

He would have experience in that.

My cell phone rang, and I grabbed it from the nightstand.

"Cookie, how would you like to go to the parade?" Dylan asked.

Well, I really wanted to look for more clues, but I suppose I should have some fun before it was time to go home. This was supposed to be like a vacation, but I'd done everything but relax since I'd arrived.

"That sounds great," I said.

"I'll pick you up in thirty minutes," Dylan said.

I wasn't sure I'd brought an outfit suitable for attending the parade, though I'd definitely want my sneakers. Sorting through my clothes, I picked out a pair of turquoise Lily Pulitzer pedal pushers from the nineties. They were embroidered with pink bumblebees. I paired them with a white

V-neck collared halter from the seventies that buttoned up the back.

While I waited for Dylan to arrive, I decided to call Heather. I couldn't wait to tell her what I'd discovered about Maureen's husband. After Heather answered, I immediately told her what I'd found out via the Ouija board.

"That certainly is shocking, if it's true."

"My grandmother has never been wrong," I said.

"I'll see what I can find out," Heather said. "How's Maureen handling the news?"

Maureen was glaring at Ramon.

"As well as can be expected, I guess. Thanks, Heather."

"No problem. I can't wait until you come back."

"Me too," I said. "Tell my mom I'll call her later."

Now I had just a little while longer to wait until Dylan arrived. I pulled out the phone from my bag. I still got a bad vibe every time I looked at it. It was as if Mandy would pop out and catch me with it. I shook off the feeling and turned on the phone. I wanted to take another look at her photos. I wanted a closer look at that bracelet.

"What are you doing?" Charlotte asked.

"Checking out something," I said.

"Good idea," she said. "I bet there are all kinds of strange things on that phone."

Now that I had a chance to enlarge the photo, I wanted a better look at the bracelet. Though I didn't get a great look at the one at the crime scene,

I suspected it was the same bracelet. I wished I had a bigger screen than my phone's to look at it on though. I used my fingers to make the screen zoom in on Danielle's wrist. The gold bracelet was much clearer now.

"What do you see?" Charlotte asked as she leaned over my shoulder.

"I'm looking closer at the bracelet. It's definitely the same as the one at the crime scene," I said.

"What kind of bracelet is it?" Maureen asked.

"A Cartier love bracelet," Charlotte and I said at the same time.

"How do you know?" Maureen asked.

"I'd know it anywhere," Charlotte said. "It's one of my favorites. I wore mine often."

"It's beautiful," I said. "I found one at an estate sale once, but after much research I discovered it wasn't authentic. Apparently back in the seventies they didn't do much to make sure that they couldn't be copied, so there were quite a few fake ones made. You have to be careful when you find one you think is vintage."

"Good information, Cookie. Now tell me something . . . how are you sure that is the bracelet that you saw?"

"I guess I don't know for sure, but I'm almost positive," I said.

"That means that Danielle was the murderer," Ramon said.

"It would seem that way," I said, still studying the picture.

I just couldn't believe that Danielle would be the murderer. I thought of her as more than a client now. She was like a friend. To think someone I trusted could be a murderer was a scary thought.

"So what do you do now?" Maureen asked.

"Well, I couldn't just accuse her based solely on this picture," I said.

"No, of course not," Charlotte said.

"What I need to do is find proof that it was hers."

"What are the odds that someone else would have such an expensive bracelet?" Charlotte asked.

"There were a lot of people who had a great deal of money at that event," I said.

"True, but how many of them would have a reason to kill Ramon?" Charlotte asked.

I turned to Ramon. "Did your wife have a bracelet like that?"

"Not that I know of, but she had a lot of little trinkets," he said.

"Trinkets?" Charlotte scoffed. "I think you'd know if she had this bracelet. It costs thousands of dollars."

He leaned in for a closer look. "For that little thing? Does it have diamonds?"

"No diamonds on this one," I said. "The one with diamonds costs tens of thousands."

"Well, I guess I didn't know everything she had."

"Safe to say he didn't buy it for her," Maureen said with disdain in her voice.

She was obviously taking her emotions out on Ramon.

"I will have to ask Danielle, although I know she will think it is a weird question," I said.

A knock sounded at my door.

"It must be Dylan," Charlotte said as she hurried over. She stuck her head out the door. "Yep. That's him. Looking handsome as usual."

I answered the door. Dylan smiled as soon as he saw me. He wore blue and brown plaid shorts, a white polo shirt, and brown loafers. I'd never seen him dressed that casually. He looked good in everything though.

"Did he do something different with his hair?" Charlotte asked.

"Is someone here?" Dylan looked over my shoulder.

For a moment, I froze.

"Oh, way to look totally suspicious," Charlotte said. "It looks like you've been caught stealing."

Dylan continued to look over my shoulder. "Were you talking to someone?"

"No." Okay, I sounded totally suspicious. "Let me grab my bag, and I'll be ready."

"You could have told him you were on the phone so he wouldn't be suspicious," Charlotte said.

Okay, Charlotte was right. I panicked though, and my brain wasn't thinking correctly. Too bad I hadn't thought of that answer. I picked up my bag and headed toward the door. Dylan was still looking around suspiciously. I closed the door so he couldn't look, although it really didn't matter. He could look all he wanted, and he'd never see the ghosts like I did.

"You look lovely, by the way," he said.

At least he was changing the subject. I couldn't believe he'd heard me talking through the door.

"Thank you. I'm excited for the parade. I've never been to one this size before. Just the small ones we have in Sugar Creek."

"It'll be fun," Dylan said.

"Any news on who the men were who could have been looking for me at the bed-and-breakfast?" I asked as we walked toward the car.

Dylan opened the door for me. "No word. I asked Hannah if she'd be willing to have an artist do a rendering of the men for me, but she declined."

"You went there to talk with her?" I asked as I buckled my seat belt.

"I wanted to get her account of what happened."

"That is so sweet of him," Charlotte said from the backseat.

"I believe it was someone who knows I've been looking into the murder," I said.

"I guess the key is to think about who knows you are looking into the murder," Dylan said as he pulled out of the parking lot.

"Well, there's Mandy. I don't know why, but I think she's suspicious of me. It's just the way she looks at me."

"But do you think she's the killer?" Dylan kept his eyes on the road.

"She's scary, but that doesn't mean she's a killer. Also, there's Danielle, Elise, and Lewis. Oh, and Ramon's wife, Kristina."

"That's kind of a long list," Dylan said.

"Unfortunately, yes, it is," I said around a sigh.

We arrived downtown and, after a bit of trying, found a parking space. Dylan and I walked over to the street where the parade would soon be going by. After a few minutes of standing in the heat and wishing I'd worn something cooler, the parade kicked off. There were marching bands, floats with various local celebrities, and cars with other local figures, plus the blow-up cartoon figures that all the children loved. I looked around for the ghosts. I think the crowd had pushed through, which meant that the ghosts were having a hard time staying beside us. When I looked over my shoulder, I spotted the three of them a little ways behind us, looking confused.

Chapter 27

Grandma Pearl's Pearls of Wisdom

Everything's better with a monogram.

"Would you like to get a lemonade?" Dylan asked. "I think it's fresh and not some powdered stuff."

"I'd love that," I said.

The stand was nearby, so we made our way through the crowd for a lemonade. The next thing I knew, the crowd grew. People shoved their way closer to the street. Dylan lost his grip on my hand. I looked around for him, but I couldn't see him in the crowd. It was as if he'd disappeared. The best thing I could do was to go to the refreshment stand. He'd probably be waiting there for me. Unfortunately, when I arrived at the stand, Dylan was nowhere in sight.

"This is ridiculous, Cookie. How did you

become lost like a child at a parade?" Charlotte was standing beside me now.

I picked up my phone and held it to my ear. "I don't know how I got lost. You saw those people shoving me. I'm lucky I didn't get trampled."

I dialed Dylan's number, but the call wouldn't go through. Apparently, there was no service in the middle of downtown. I seriously needed to reconsider my cell phone provider. Dylan was probably trying to call me too.

I released a big sigh and continued to scan the crowd of faces for Dylan. That was when I noticed the men. At that same moment, they spotted me. Our eyes met. I took off running, trying to make my way through the crowd, but people weren't cooperating and stood in my way. Some people even shoved me as I tried to break through. It looked as if I wasn't going to get away from the men.

When I glanced back, the men were still trying to get to me. I had to find a place to hide so they wouldn't find me. I figured the crowd would be enough to keep me separated from them, but somehow the men were keeping up with me. When I reached a line of shiny new cars parked along the street, I decided to hide behind one of them.

"You should see if the door is unlocked, Cookie. The windows are down. You can hide in the backseat," Charlotte suggested.

I reached up and tried the handle. The door was open. Could I really hide back there?

"Someone will think I'm trying to steal the car," I whispered.

"You'll only be there a minute," Charlotte said.

"It probably won't be necessary to stay. I think they're gone," Maureen said.

"Not so fast. Here they come now," Ramon yelled.

I pulled on the door handle, opened it, and crawled into the backseat. Once I was all the way in, I closed it behind me. I couldn't believe I was hiding in someone's car. What would Dylan say? I knew he was looking for me. The ghosts were standing guard outside the car.

"What's happening now?" I asked.

"Here comes a man. Hold on," Charlotte said.

The next thing I knew, the front driver's-side door opened and a man got in the car. Fortunately, he hadn't looked in the backseat yet to see me lying there. He cranked the engine and shoved the car into gear. I didn't know what to do. I was paralyzed. Should I let him know I was back there? I don't know what he would do, but if I didn't say something, there was no telling where he would drive me.

Things had happened so fast that the ghosts barely had time to register that I was gone. I'd never left them that quickly, and I just assumed they would be able to keep up with me. That didn't happen this time. They would think I had left them on purpose. In my defense, getting into the backseat had been Charlotte's idea. The car slowed down, but we were still moving. The car was going no more than five miles an hour. Cheers from the crowd filled the air. The parade was under way.

I wanted to look out to see where we were. I eased my way over to the window. So far, the driver still had no idea I was back there. When I looked out the window, I realized I was in the parade. The car was part of the parade. The crowd was cheering. I wasn't sure if they saw me peeking out the back window. Suddenly I made eye contact with someone. I was looking right at Dylan, and he was looking back at me. I'd never seen that expression on his face before—it was one of complete and utter shock.

Would he believe me when I told him that I just felt like being part of the Kentucky Derby Pegasus Parade? The man glanced back and saw me.

"What the heck are you doing back there?" he asked. "Who are you?"

I knew my answer would sound completely crazy. "You see, sir, there were two men following me, so I had to get away from them. I jumped in the backseat of your car so they wouldn't find me."

"You can't be back there." The man's loud voice boomed through the car.

"Well, it's a little too late for that now," I said, sitting up in the backseat.

I waved at the crowd as we drove by.

"You're not part of the parade," he said.

"It looks more suspicious if I don't wave to people."

People were waving at me now.

"How am I going to explain this?" he said.

"Just tell them the truth, I guess."

We continued down the street. I made eye contact with the ghosts. Their mouths hung open as they stared in shock. After the parade had progressed several more streets, the man pulled over.

"Are you going to leave me here?"

"You're lucky I didn't call the police."

I wished he had. At least I'd lost the men. Now I had to find Dylan. After getting out of the car, I stood on the sidewalk, staring at the tall buildings of downtown Louisville. Everything was closed for the day. My cell phone rang. Thank goodness, I had service again.

"Where are you?" Dylan asked.

"It's a long story, but I need you to pick me up."

Chapter 28

Cookie's Savvy Tips for Vintage Shopping

*If you have the time while traveling,
make sure to check out local vintage and thrift shops.
You never know what treasures you may find.*

After my ordeal at the parade, I'd had Dylan drop me off at the hotel so I could rest. My stress level was at the max. A couple of hours had passed, and I'd gone out to find a snack at the store around the corner. The rest of the evening, I planned on relaxing in front of the TV and writing for my blog. That always eased my tension.

I pulled into the hotel's parking lot and around to the back, where I parked my car close to my room. I liked to get that spot because I could look out the window and keep an eye on my car. I didn't want anyone messing around with my baby. As I backed the car in, I noticed a black truck parked not too far away underneath a big shade tree.

"Do you see that?" I asked the ghosts. "Underneath that tree?"

"It's that truck," Charlotte said.

"Yes, and I don't think it's a coincidence. The person is waiting for me," I said.

"I'm going over to find out what they're doing," Charlotte said.

Before I had a chance to say anything, she was gone. Not that I would have stopped her. Actually, I was glad that she was going. I turned off the car and waited until Charlotte returned before getting out. If the situation escalated, I might have to drive off. I'd call Dylan and have him meet me here with the police.

A few seconds later, Charlotte returned.

"What did you find out?" I asked.

"There's a woman in the truck. She was on her phone, and I'm pretty sure she was talking to Mandy. She hung up not long after I got in the truck."

"That was unfortunate timing," Maureen said.

"You should go over there and confront her." Charlotte shook her fist.

"Oh, that sounds dangerous." Maureen's eyes widened.

"That's because it is dangerous," Ramon said. "If it has anything to do with Mandy, I would never confront her."

I tapped my fingers against the steering wheel,

contemplating whether I should go over to find out what this woman wanted. I weighed the pros and cons of doing that. She could want to fight me or even worse. I was pretty sure she had tried to cut me off so that I'd have an accident. Plus, she had tried to run over me with her truck.

"Okay, I'll do it," I said, opening the car door.

I had to go now before I changed my mind. I moved over to the side lot, close to the building. I wanted to conceal my presence so that she wouldn't know I was walking up to her truck, although she was probably waiting for me. That was her entire reason for being there. She hadn't been paying enough attention, though, to even realize that I'd pulled into the parking lot. The closer I got to the truck, the more my nerves ramped up. With the tinted windows on the truck, it was impossible to see what she was doing.

I pushed my shoulders back and stood up a little straighter as I marched over to the truck.

"Go get her, Cookie," Charlotte said.

"Just be careful," Maureen added.

"I would go ahead and punch nine one one into your phone if I were you," Ramon said.

I stepped up to the truck and knocked on the window. The woman didn't lower the window or open the door. The windows were tinted, but now that I was closer, I could make out her silhouette. I knew she was there. I wasn't going to give up, and I wasn't going away until I talked to her.

After a pause, she cracked the window and glared at me. "What do you want?"

She had blond hair that reached to her shoulders in waves. She wasn't as gaunt-looking as Mandy. This woman had fuller features.

"What do *I* want?" I asked. "More like what do you want?" I placed my hands on my hips. "You're the one who's been following me. I want an answer. I want to know why you've been following me."

"Mandy. That's why I'm following you. I want to put a stop to it," she said as she opened the truck door and got out.

She was several inches taller than me. I looked up, and she peered down at me like a giant oak tree towering over a tiny acorn.

"Mandy is my best friend, and I'm looking out for her." She stepped closer.

"Yeah, I know this lady," Ramon said. "Her name is April. She's crazy. You should leave now, Cookie, before this gets any worse."

The only way it could get worse was if she actually punched me, and it looked like that was where this was headed.

"I'm not following Mandy. All I ever see is your truck and you trying to run over me," I said.

"Yeah, I will get you if you get in my way again. I'll do it all over again. You can take this as a warning." She reached out and pushed my shoulder.

I stumbled backward.

"Okay, it's definitely time to leave," Maureen said.

I should have left, but this just made me even angrier. I pushed April's shoulder in return. Of course, she didn't stumble backward as I had. My shove had absolutely zero effect on her, as if I had tried to push a brick wall. Did she lift weights?

"It's like a Chihuahua fighting a pit bull," Charlotte said.

"Cookie, this will not end well for you," Maureen said.

"You're the Chihuahua, remember?" Charlotte said.

Maybe so, but I knew some Chihuahuas who stood up for themselves. That being said, I wasn't completely crazy, so I told April to leave me alone. I turned around and stomped away.

"Is she following me?" I whispered.

I didn't want to turn around and let her know I was scared.

"No, she got back in her truck," Ramon said.

"You were brave, Cookie. I'm proud of you." Charlotte smiled.

As soon as I walked into my room, my phone rang. I looked at the screen and saw that it was my mother's number. I picked it up right away because I knew she would be frantic if I didn't answer.

"Cookie, how are you, honey?"

My mom sometimes still treated me like I was six years old, but that was okay. She was a great mother, and if it made her happy, I was okay with it.

"I'm all right. Is everything okay? How's Dad?"

"Well, it's hard since I'm away from him and staying here in Sugar Creek. He came over to see me a couple of nights ago."

"Stop right there. I don't want to hear anything about that visit. Is anything else going on?" I asked.

She chuckled. "Well, the real reason I'm calling is because I'm concerned about Heather."

"What's wrong with Heather?" I asked.

"I know she wouldn't tell you this, so that's why I felt the need to do it. Someone has been following her."

"What do you mean following her? Who is it?" I asked, with concern evident in my voice.

"I think it might be related to the murder case. I think the person who killed Maureen is following Heather. She might be onto them, and they're worried that she'll go to the police."

Heather was being followed? Now I had a sick feeling in my stomach. I never wanted to drag any of my friends or family into my investigations. It looked as if I had done it with Heather this time.

"Has she told the police about this?" I asked.

"Well, no, I don't think she has said anything yet. I don't even think she knows that I know."

"Maybe you should tell the police," I said.

"I thought perhaps you could tell Dylan, and he could share it with some of his colleagues."

"Sure, I can do that," I said. "Have you gotten any clues on who this might be? You actually think it might be the killer?"

"We have some suspects, like Maureen's husband and the woman he was having an affair with. There are also some of Maureen's neighbors. They had had an argument over some kind of meeting that Maureen was in charge of."

"I can have Dylan look into all of those people," I said.

"That's a good idea, Cookie, and in the meantime, I'll try to keep an eye on Heather."

"Just be safe, Mom," I said. "Now I'm worried about you too. Maybe I need to come home."

"No, that's not necessary. I can take care of myself, and we won't let anything happen to Heather."

"All right," I said around a sigh. "But I'm telling Dylan, and we'll get to the bottom of this right away."

"I know you will, darling. I'll talk to you soon."

"I'll be home soon."

"That didn't sound like a good call," Charlotte said.

The ghosts stared at me. I knew they were looking for any sign of trouble on my face.

"No, everything's fine." I forced a smile.

I didn't want Maureen to worry. She would think that she was the one responsible if anything happened to any of my friends or family. I picked up the phone and dialed Heather, but she didn't answer. It went straight to her voice mail, which was kind of odd because she always picked up when I called. I left a message and told her to call me back. I hoped that she did soon. Although now that I thought about it, I didn't know if I should tell her what my mother had said. She really should know.

After I hung up the phone, the ghosts were staring at me. I was pretty sure they were suspicious. When Heather called back, I would have to get away from them for a moment so that I could tell her what my mother had shared.

Chapter 29

Grandma Pearl's Pearls of Wisdom

Stay classy and sassy.

I'd been out running a few last-minute errands, grabbing things for Danielle's Derby Day outfit. As I headed down the sidewalk toward my car, my phone rang. I recognized Ken's number. I hoped nothing was wrong. I picked up the phone.

"Hey, Cookie, I was wondering if you had time to meet me?"

Since I had been kind of putting him off the entire trip, I figured we should talk a bit.

"Sure, where would you like to meet?" I asked.

"How about we meet over at this place called The Bourbon Bar that I just passed. I can get you the address," he said.

"Yeah, sure, that'll be great." I took down the address and hurried into the Buick.

"I love bourbon," Ramon said from the backseat.

The place was just a few streets over, so it only took a couple of minutes to get there, even with the traffic. After finding a parking spot, I put money into the meter and walked into the restaurant. It was called The Bourbon Bar, but it was actually a restaurant. The walls were lined with rich wooden shelves holding bourbon bottles. They looked like soldiers in formation. A long bar was at the right, and tables were grouped to the left. It didn't look as if there was a single table available. When I looked across the room, I spotted Ken. He waved me over to a table in the corner.

"It's dark in here," Maureen said. "I can barely see where I'm going."

"It's called mood lighting," Charlotte said.

Ken pushed to his feet and then pulled out the chair for me. "What do you think of the place? Are you ready for some bourbon?"

I sat down and picked up the menu. "I'm not sure about bourbon at this time of day. However, I think I'd like to try this blackberry-and-bourbon cobbler."

Ken laughed. "That sounds like a good plan."

When the waiter arrived, we placed our orders. I ordered the bourbon-glazed turkey sandwich with sautéed vegetables, and Ken ordered the barbequed sliced brisket. While we waited for the food, we discussed our Kentucky trips so far and the upcoming Derby. Luckily, Ken hadn't mentioned anything about Dylan or anything related to our current situation. After a few minutes, our food arrived. While eating, we continued our chitchat. Conversations were always easy with Ken.

After we finished, Ken picked up the check.

"You don't have to do that," I said.

He looked me in the eyes. "I want to."

"Well, okay. Thank you," I said.

"What about we go on this tour that I just saw?"

"What kind of tour?" I asked.

"It's for historic homes in town. Apparently, they have amazing historic homes here."

Wow. I really did want to see that.

"Okay, what time does it start?" I asked.

"In half an hour. We would have just enough time to get over there. It's within walking distance."

Charlotte stood between us. Ken of course had no idea. "That sounds perfect."

Ken paid for the food, and we headed down the street toward the tour.

"He sure is enjoying your company, Cookie," Charlotte said.

She didn't need to tell me that. I was enjoying his company too. Why did things have to be so complicated? I went forever without having any prospects of a date, and now there were two men in my life.

Soon we reached the building where we would purchase the tickets and where the tour would start. Ken purchased our tickets while I waited on the sidewalk with the ghosts. There was a bright blue cloudless sky and a gentle breeze; it was a perfect day for a walking tour.

"Don't you think you should tell Dylan what you're doing?" Ramon quirked an eyebrow.

"You be quiet." Maureen waved her finger. "I know what you're trying to do."

The tour guide led the way down the sidewalk. Ken and I walked side by side down the sidewalk, looking at the grand Victorian homes.

"My name is David Domine," the handsome blond tour guide said. "Follow me as I lead you through one of the most architecturally exuberant neighborhoods in the country."

We followed along, clinging to his every word. Even the ghosts were enthralled.

"Construction of the homes started in the eighteen eighties," David said. "Styles included Châteauesque, Richardsonian-Romanesque, Italianate, Victorian Gothic, and Queen Anne."

I peered up at the magnificent structures. All of the mansions were well taken care of. It was almost like stepping back in time. I almost expected to see men and women in period dress. Trees lined the sidewalks, and even though there was traffic and noise, it was still an enjoyable time. Amazingly, the ghosts were being quiet and enjoying the narration of the tour. In spite of having a good time, I couldn't help but feel like someone was watching us. I turned around several times, but the people behind us were just listening to the tour and not really paying attention to us.

As we stood in front of one of the grand homes, I looked across the way and saw the two men— the ones who had followed me at the parade and, I assumed, the ones who had shown up at the bed-and-breakfast. This wasn't a coincidence.

I touched Ken's arm. "Do you see those men over there?"

Ken followed my pointing finger. "Yes."

"Those guys are the ones I think were at the bed-and-breakfast."

Charlotte pointed. "That's them, Cookie. Do something."

Ken looked at me. "What makes you think that?"

"They followed me at the parade too," I said.

When the men realized we were watching them, they turned around and walked away.

"I don't want to let them get away," Ken said. "We need to follow them."

"Yes, that's it. Follow them." Charlotte gestured for us to hurry.

"They're getting away," Maureen said.

"Follow them? Are you sure? That sounds kind of terrifying," I said.

"Well, I'm going to ask what they're doing, so I have to. I really don't want to leave you here alone."

I nodded. "Let's go."

We broke free from the group and headed across the park area, trailing behind the men. They glanced back and quickened their steps. We had to hurry to keep up, but ultimately, they reached a white truck and jumped in quickly. The guy cranked the truck and took off.

"Wow, they were in a hurry," I said.

"Did you get a good look at the truck?" Ken asked.

"I saw what was written on the side."

"Really? What was that?" Ken asked.

"Churchill Downs," I said.

"It's just too bizarre, Cookie," Charlotte said.

Did Ramon recognize the men? I supposed he wouldn't know everyone who worked at Churchill Downs.

"What are we doing now?" I asked. "How will we find out who they are?"

"I'll check around. I think I can get some information out of Churchill Downs, especially since they were driving a company truck. Not to mention that they followed you and threatened Hannah."

"Good thinking, Ken," Maureen said.

Ken placed his hand on the small of my back and helped me cross the pebbled path. "For now, we can leave. It doesn't look like they're coming back."

"I'm glad," I said. "I never want to see them again."

I just hoped that Ken could find out some information on them. I wanted to put a stop to whatever they were up to.

A couple minutes later, we fell back into the tour. The guide hadn't seemed to notice that we were gone. We'd had to hurry down the sidewalk a bit to catch up with them, but we hadn't missed too much. Of course, I was on the lookout for the men for the rest of the tour. Once the tour was complete, we headed back to my car.

"I'm glad that you enjoyed our time together today," Ken said as we stepped beside my car.

"This was a date, Cookie," Maureen said.

The ghosts were leaning against my old Buick, watching us.

"Just in case you didn't know," Charlotte added.

I hadn't thought of it at the time, but I suppose one could classify this as a date. I just figured it was two friends hanging out. Dylan might see it differently though. Now I felt terrible. I hadn't even thought of it as a date. Had Ken thought it was a date?

After Ken kissed me on the cheek, he took off for his car.

"Not a date, huh?" Ramon leaned forward from the backseat and propped his arms on the back of my seat.

"Leave her alone." Maureen waved her hand at Ramon.

After starting the car, I glanced over. That was when I realized that I'd left my car unlocked. There was a note on the seat beside me. I reached down and picked it up. This was definitely a note and not just a receipt that had fallen out of my purse. I'd read only a couple of words when I realized that it was some kind of a strange poem, or at least an attempt at a poem. Had Mandy left this?

I looked around to see if I could spot anyone who might have left it, but there was no telling how long it had been there. Someone could have left it right after I went into The Bourbon Bar.

Chapter 30

Cookie's Savvy Tips for Vintage Shopping

*Wearing a vintage piece
that was once trendy is a great way
to add new flair to your modern outfits.*

Later that evening, I received a text message. I didn't recognize the number. Whoever had sent it asked me to come to the barn. I replied, asking who had sent the text, but I got no further messages.

"That seems odd, Cookie. I don't think you should go," Maureen said.

"You might as well be talking to a wall, Maureen. This is Cookie Chanel, and she doesn't always do the wisest things," Charlotte said.

"Oh, and you're one to talk," I said. "Like you always did the best things."

"Exactly my point. I made a lot of mistakes, and I'm just trying to make sure you learn from my mistakes."

"I understand, Charlotte, but this seems too important to pass up. What if it's from Danielle? After all, she is paying for me to be here. If she needs my help, I should go there."

"Well, she could also be the killer," Charlotte said.

"Yes, there is that, but I still don't think she could do such a thing."

"Look, the car is already headed in that direction. I don't think she's going to listen to you all, ladies," Ramon said.

Soon I had arrived at the barn. Normally things would have been quiet at this time of day, but with the Derby hours away, the place was busy with activity.

I parked the car and hurried over toward the barn. When I stepped around the side, there was no one there, only the horses. If only they could talk. I looked around for a minute but still couldn't find anyone. I sent a message to the number that had texted me, but I received no further messages. I dialed Danielle's number to ask if it was her. She didn't answer, so I left a message.

"This is weird. I knew I had a bad feeling about this place," Maureen said.

"I'll just look around a little more, and we can leave," I said.

I stepped over to the office door and knocked. No one answered, but I hadn't really expected that anyway. I twisted the doorknob, and to my surprise, it opened.

"What are you doing, Cookie?" Charlotte asked.

"I didn't expect the door to be unlocked."

"Why did you try it in the first place?" she asked.

"I was curious." I peeked into the room and called out. No one answered. "I wonder why the door is open."

"I guess someone forgot to lock it," Charlotte said.

I eased the door open a little more and stepped inside the room.

"What are you doing?" Charlotte whispered, as if someone would hear her.

"I just want to take a little look around," I said.

"See, she is out of control," Maureen said. "She starts out nervous about snooping, and now she is addicted to it."

"I am not addicted, but I've decided that if I really want to solve this case I have to take a few risks." I looked around the room.

"This is a huge risk," Ramon said.

"What do you think you're looking for?" Charlotte asked.

"I'm not sure. Nothing, I suppose."

"Let's get out of here," Maureen insisted.

I went over to the desk and sifted through the drawers.

"I don't know if this is such a good idea," Maureen said.

"Oh, she won't get caught. It will be okay," Charlotte said with a wave of her hand.

When I pulled out the drawer on the far right, I noticed something at the bottom. It looked as if the drawer was lifted up slightly at the bottom. I picked at the edge and got the piece to come up.

"What is that?" Ramon asked.

"It looked like a secret compartment," Charlotte said.

"That's exactly what it is," I said.

"What's in there?" Maureen asked.

"All I see is a bottle of something."

"Well, get it out and see what it is," Charlotte said.

I pulled the bottle out. It was a clear bottle with clear liquid. There was a label across the front. Of course, I didn't really understand what it meant or was for.

"That's the stuff they give to the horses," Ramon said.

Charlotte and I exchanged a look.

"Like what they say was given to you?" I asked.

Ramon stared at me as if he didn't know what to say.

"I think we're on to something," Maureen said. "This doesn't look good, Cookie. What are you going to do?"

"I don't know what to do." I pulled out my phone and took a photo of the medicine bottle. "I can't take it with me. I don't even like that I picked the thing up."

"You have to tell the police. I think we've found the killer," Maureen said.

"You think it was Elise?" I asked. "Just because the bottle was found here doesn't prove that she did it."

"Why else would she have the medicine?"

"Doesn't she give it to the horse?"

"No, only a vet would do that," Ramon said.

"Maybe someone planted it here."

"Why would they do that?" Charlotte asked.

"Maybe they wanted it to look as if Elise had done this," I said.

"So we're no closer to finding the killer?" Maureen asked.

"Maybe a little closer, but we're far from solving the case just yet."

Voices sounded, as if someone was nearing the office.

"Someone's coming. You have to get out of here," Charlotte said in a panic.

I tossed the bottle back into the drawer and replaced the liner that had covered the opening. At least I had a photo of the thing. I would show Dylan, and then we could go to the police with the info. I closed the drawer and jumped up from the seat. Once by the door, I paused. The voices were still nearby, but I had no idea if the person was coming into the office.

"What are you going to do?" Ramon asked.

"She's going to get out of here, that's what. Leave now, Cookie." Charlotte gestured as if she was trying to push me.

I eased the door open and peeked out. Thank goodness, I didn't see anyone, but I knew they were nearby. I had to hurry before someone caught me. If Elise really was the killer and she caught me in her office, what would she do? Would I be the next victim? I stepped out of the office, pulled the door behind me, and rushed down the aisle away from the door. At least now if someone spotted me, I could pretend I had just arrived.

"That was a close one, Cookie," Charlotte said.

"I told you she'd get caught." Maureen said.

"Well, she wasn't caught. Just almost caught," Charlotte corrected.

When I headed around the side of the barn, I noticed Elise. She was walking in the same direction, so her back was facing me. She had something in her hand, but I couldn't tell what it was. After a few seconds, she tossed it on the ground. She kicked a nearby bucket.

"Wow, she seems pretty angry," Maureen said.

She kept walking, so I went up to the spot where she had tossed the thing to see what she'd left.

"Well, it's nothing special that would solve the murder case," Maureen said.

Elise had tossed down the horse's reins. That wasn't a clue for anything, but she was angry, so I continued to follow her. She moved over to another barn and out of my sight. I hurried my steps so that I could catch up with her. When I peeked around the side of the barn, I spotted her. She had stopped by a white truck. It was marked with "Churchill Downs" on the side of the door.

"Is she meeting someone?" Charlotte asked.

"It looks that way," I said.

As long as Elise couldn't see me, I would stand there and wait for whoever was meeting her. I caught movement out of the corner of my eye. From the opposite direction, I spotted Lewis.

"Oh, he must be meeting her," Maureen said.

Elise and Lewis stood next to each other beside the truck. They were talking. I really wished I could hear what they were saying.

"You should move closer, Cookie," Charlotte said. "You want to find out what they're talking about."

I decided to take Charlotte's advice and move closer. How would I go undetected? I didn't want Elise or Lewis to see me. There were a few trees nearby, so if I could get over to one of them, I'd be able to hide, and they wouldn't see me.

"I can cause a distraction," Charlotte said. "That way they'll look in the opposite direction, and you can hurry over to the trees."

I nodded. "That sounds like a good plan. What are you going to do to distract them?"

"I'll just throw a rock or something."

"Can you do that?" I asked.

"I can if I focus all of my energy. I'll be drained for the rest of the day, so I might not be able to talk much."

I quirked an eyebrow. Hey, why hadn't I thought of that sooner?

"I know what you're thinking, Cookie, and that's not nice." Charlotte placed her hands on her hips.

"Never mind that. Let's do it," I said.

Charlotte did exactly as she had said. She managed to toss a rock just a bit. That caught their attention. Elise and Lewis stepped over a bit toward the area where the rock had landed. I knew they'd never figure out what had made the noise. In the meantime, I had my chance to run. Now I was hiding behind an oak tree.

"I don't know what that was," Elise said.

"Well, regardless, back to our conversation," Lewis said.

"Now we're getting to the good stuff." Maureen rubbed her hands together.

"I realize what you think, Elise, but I just don't want anyone to know what we've been doing."

My eyes widened.

Lewis continued talking. "We'll just keep it quiet. No one will have to know."

I exchanged a look with the ghosts. What did Lewis mean by that?

"That sounds pretty ominous," Maureen said.

"I told you he wasn't a nice guy," Ramon said.

"Well, we don't have evidence that he did anything wrong just yet, but I have to admit that sounds pretty incriminating," I said.

Their voices were still low. I moved forward so that I could possibly hear more clearly. That was when I stumbled on a tree root. I reached for the trunk and somehow managed to catch myself. Unfortunately, a loud groan escaped my lips in the process. Lewis and Elise looked around. My cover was blown. I couldn't act as if they hadn't seen me, so I just tossed my hand up and smiled.

"I'm just passing through," I said.

They looked at me strangely at first, but ultimately, they waved and smiled in return.

"Do you think they believed me? Are they suspicious?" I asked.

"I think anyone would be suspicious of that," Charlotte said.

Once back at the hotel, I picked up my phone and dialed Heather's number. I needed to find out if she'd discovered any new information about Maureen's death.

"Magic Marketplace. This is Heather, making your magical dreams come true. How may I help you?"

"When did you add that new slogan?" I asked.

"Oh, I just thought of it this morning. Do you like it?" Heather asked.

I knew by the tone of her voice that she was smiling.

"It's interesting," I said.

"You don't like it," Heather said.

"I just think maybe you need something a little more mysterious to go with the theme of your shop."

"Ugh. You're right. I sounded like an occult cheerleader—way too peppy. I knew I could count on you to tell me the truth."

"That's what friends are for," I said. "How's everything in Sugar Creek?"

"Things are great. I sold that blue Dior gown."

"Wow. You're doing such a great job," I said. "How can I thank you?"

"Chocolate cake?"

I laughed. "Sure."

"What about you? How's Kentucky?" Heather asked.

"Hectic, I guess."

"Any news on the murder?" she asked.

"Nothing new. What about there? Any clues about Maureen?" I asked.

"Actually, I was just getting ready to call you."

I knew Heather was easily distracted.

"I found out where Maureen died."

"Really? Where?" I asked.

"At her home. In the kitchen while she was baking a cake."

Maureen's gaze was focused on me.

"You're talking about me," she said. "What is she saying?"

"How long ago did this happen?" I asked.

Maureen had never told me how long she'd been a ghost.

"This happened several years ago."

"How tragic," I said.

"Cookie, please don't keep us in suspense," Charlotte said as she paced in front of me.

I had just a few more questions for Heather, and then I'd give the ghosts all the details.

My next question was a difficult one. "Heather, do you know how it happened?"

Charlotte froze in front of me. She knew what I was asking.

"Actually, yes, I do. Maureen was strangled. They found the rope at the scene."

Suddenly I felt as if I couldn't breathe.

"Are you okay?" Heather asked.

"This doesn't sound like good news," Maureen said. "I'd better sit down."

Who would do such a thing to Maureen?

"How did you find out this information?" I asked.

"Turns out your mother was persuasive with the police."

"Did she offer them cookies?" I asked.

"Yes, the chickpea ones."

"No wonder the police talked."

"I think they're considering adding her to the force," Heather said.

I laughed.

"Do they have any leads on who may have done it?"

"They believe it was someone Maureen knew. There were no signs of forced entry."

"But it wasn't the husband?"

"Of course not," Maureen answered.

"I don't know," Heather said. "I have a customer. I'll call you soon."

"Make their magical dreams come true," I said with a laugh.

"Ugh," Heather said.

Charlotte and Maureen stood in front of me with their arms crossed in front of their chests. They tapped their feet against the floor.

"Well?" Charlotte said.

"Maureen was murdered in her house. Someone strangled her."

Maureen plopped down in the chair next to the window. She stared straight ahead and said, "I can't believe this."

"It will take a while for it to sink in. She'll be okay after a bit," Charlotte said.

I grabbed my bag. "Let's go."

"Where are we going?" Charlotte asked.

"I want to find the horse groomer who disappeared. Plus, I think we should go to Dr. Rivere's house."

"Good idea. I think she might hold a clue," Maureen said as she followed me.

I was on my way to Dr. Rivere's home so that I could ask her questions personally. Luckily, I had found her address. Twenty minutes later, I pulled up in front of the beautiful, two-story brick house. The ghosts followed me out of the car and to the front door.

"Don't mess this up, Cookie," Charlotte said.

"What is that supposed to mean? I can't ask questions?"

"Just don't make her suspicious so that she won't answer your questions."

I rang the doorbell, but no one came to the door. I pushed it again, but still no one opened the door. Reluctantly, I decided to give up. Apparently, she wasn't home.

"What do you think's going on?"

"I don't know. She wasn't at her work, and now she's not at home."

"That's a little concerning," Maureen said.

"Yes, and she's not the only one who is missing. Corbin the groomer hasn't been around either," I said.

"Do you think their disappearance could have something to do with my murder?" Ramon asked.

"Anything is possible." I moved away from the door.

Before I reached the car, a woman was waving at me from the house next door.

"Are you here to see Dr. Rivere?" she asked.

"Yes, I'm here to see her."

"Are you a friend of hers?" She looked me up and down.

"No, we're . . . I mean, I just need to ask her a few questions."

"Something happened to her, didn't it? I knew something happened." The neighbor seemed upset.

"What do you mean?" I asked.

"She usually stops by to see me every couple of days. When I didn't see her, I went over to check. She didn't answer. Like I said, she usually stops by to see how I'm doing or just to say hi."

"But she hasn't lately?" I asked.

"Not for a couple days," the woman said.

"And you live in this house?" I pointed.

"Yes, this is my home. Are you a detective?"

"She should be," Maureen said.

"No. Like I said, I'm just a friend."

Charlotte scoffed. "You're such a liar. Whatever

it takes to solve the case though. I'm proud of you, Cookie."

"Do you think she's okay?" the neighbor asked.

"I think she's fine." I handed her a card. "You'll call me if you hear from her?"

"Absolutely." She took the card.

"This just keeps getting weirder," Charlotte said as she got into the car.

I turned the ignition and pulled away from the curb. "Now to Corbin's."

I'd gotten Corbin's address and decided to check out his house too. Like Ramon said, I knew that Corbin's disappearance had something to do with Ramon's murder.

"Are you sure you know where you're going?" Charlotte asked as I turned left.

"No, what made you think I know where I'm going."

"Cookie, you should use a map," Maureen said.

"I'm using the navigation on my phone, but that still doesn't mean I know where I'm going." I slowed down to look at the street sign.

"Edgewood Drive. That's where I'm going. See, I didn't get lost." I counted down the houses

"It sure doesn't look as if anyone is home," Charlotte said.

The only light cutting through the dark night came from the streetlights and the nearby homes. Corbin's address was dark and quiet.

I stepped out of the car. "It looks as if he hasn't returned either."

"Maybe Corbin and the doctor are together," Maureen said.

"Together in a shallow grave dug by the killer," Charlotte said under her breath.

"Don't talk like that when I'm walking out here in the dark by myself," I whispered.

"Just telling the truth. You should always be on guard."

I eased up onto the porch. I was seriously having thoughts of running back to my car. Pushing back my doubts, I got up enough courage to knock on the door.

"He's not there," a male voice said.

I jumped and clutched my chest.

"Who said that?" Charlotte spun around.

"Over here," the man said.

I looked to the right and spotted a man sitting on the front porch of the house next door.

"Looking for Corbin?" he asked.

"Yes. Have you seen him?"

"Are you a cop?"

"Why does everyone think Cookie is a cop?" Charlotte asked.

"No, just a friend," I said as I stepped closer to the man's porch.

"He took off. He didn't say where he was going."

"Do you know why?" I asked.

The man leaned back in his rocker. "Not exactly, but I heard someone was after him."

"After him? What do you mean?"

"I mean someone was trying to hurt him."

"But you don't know who?" I asked.

He rocked back and forth. "No, and I hope I don't find out."

The longer I stood out there in the dark, the spookier it got.

"Thank you," I said.

It was time for me to get back to the hotel. I got the strange sensation that I was being watched.

Chapter 31

Grandma Pearl's Pearls of Wisdom

Never underestimate the power of a hissy fit.

The day had arrived for the Derby. Dylan was picking me up, and we'd ride together. Lewis had invited Ken to be a guest at his table, along with me and Dylan, so I knew I'd see him there. I was fine with that, but I didn't know how Dylan would react. I wondered if he'd think that I had arranged for Ken to be at the table with us. I supposed it would be a bit awkward. Dylan had given the information to the police about the drugs I'd seen in Elise's office. I still wasn't sure what excuse he'd given for how I'd found them. He was concerned about my snooping, but he didn't know the half of it.

"You'd better hurry, Cookie, or you'll be late," Charlotte said.

I'd decided on a red dress with a white floral

pattern. Actually, it matched the red roses of the
Derby. My strapless Givenchy dress was white
brocade silk with golden floral embroidery. It had
a fitted waist and a bell skirt that hit just above the
knees. My wide-brimmed hat was white with a
cluster of red roses on the side. My gold Gucci
wedge heels and matching bag finished the look.
I didn't want to be too matchy-matchy. Dylan wore
a light beige Hugo Boss suit with a vintage light
blue Hermès tie and crisp white shirt. I'd picked
out the tie. I didn't want us to be the coordinated
couple.

We had to park far away from the action and
catch a shuttle to the track. The twin spires were
visible from a good distance away. The excitement
was hard to describe, but it definitely swirled in the
air. The crowd grew larger the closer we got to
the entrance. The historic section was evident—a
brick floor and old structures that were surrounded
by new additions. Once we gave the attendant our
tickets, we were directed to the elevators that
would take us to the upper level. It felt as if we
were being escorted into a secret FBI room.

Once at the top, we were guided to the assigned
table. Everyone was already seated. Lewis and
his wife. Elise and her husband. Danielle and her
husband were there too. Mandy was down at
the paddocks with the horse, preparing for the
big race.

There was a lot to take in at the track. With so
many people and excitement, for a brief time I
forgot about the ghosts next to me and the murder

investigation. But when Charlotte started excitedly pointing out celebrities, I was yanked back to reality. But I couldn't acknowledge her and remind her not to get so excited. Maybe I could slip away and let her gain her composure. I had no idea she would get so excited about seeing Joey Fatone. I mean, I had liked some of NSYNC's songs, but I didn't like them that much.

I wasn't expecting to see Kristina at the Derby. She looked at me when she walked by. The smirk on her face told me she wasn't happy with me. She wore a white sleeveless dress that had a multi-colored floral pattern. Her yellow hat was so big that it looked as if she might tip forward from the weight.

Dylan hadn't mentioned what had happened with her. The last time I asked, he said he was working on getting the information. Apparently, the police had released her. That didn't mean she wasn't the killer though. I touched Dylan's arm.

When he looked at me, I motioned with a tilt of my head. That was when he spotted Kristina. Before he even had a chance to speak, his phone alerted him to a text message. After Dylan read the screen, he showed it to me. The message was from the detective Dylan had been talking to about the case.

"She was just released this morning. I guess because they didn't have enough evidence," Dylan said.

"Just in time for her to make the Derby," I said.

I didn't think Ramon had even noticed her yet.

He was standing a short distance away, talking with Charlotte and Maureen. It looked as if they were plotting something. Whatever it was, it couldn't be good.

Dylan had been talking with Elise's husband. I looked down the long table. Ken was sitting at the other end beside Lewis. We made eye contact, and he smiled. He really was a sweet guy.

I was thrilled that the outfits I'd picked out had turned out fabulously. Even though I was having fun, a dark cloud hung over the event because of the murder. Nothing felt safe. It was as if I was waiting for a storm to hit.

Since Charlotte was still stalking the celebrities, I had to get her out of the room and talk with her. I pushed to my feet. Dylan got up too.

"If you'll excuse me, I'm going to the ladies' room."

"Do you need me to help guide you through the crowd?" Dylan asked.

"Such a sweet offer," Maureen said. "Some guys are nice." She shot daggers at Ramon with her eyes.

"I'll be okay," I said with a smile.

Dylan seemed a bit nervous, but he smiled in return.

"I won't be long."

I weaved through the crowd and eventually came to the ladies' room.

"Wow, look at the line." Charlotte pointed.

There was no way I was waiting on that line. Besides, I wouldn't be able to talk with Charlotte and the ghosts privately there anyway. There had to be somewhere else to go.

I turned around and headed down the hallway. That was when I spotted Mandy. Her back was facing me, so I didn't think she'd seen me. What was she doing up here? They said she was down at the paddocks with the horse, waiting for the race.

"You should follow her," Charlotte said.

"Dylan will be upset if you don't come back soon," Ramon said.

"He probably noticed that line when we came in, so I think he knows it will be a while," I said.

I would follow her for just a bit to see where she was going. Maybe she was looking for Lewis.

"I hope she doesn't see you," Ramon said.

I followed Mandy down the hall. When she got on the elevator, I had to wait. I couldn't follow her into the elevator.

"There are stairs." Charlotte pointed. "If you hurry, you can beat the elevator."

"In these shoes?"

I wasn't sure hurrying was an option, but I decided to give it a shot. There was no way I would catch Mandy if I had to wait for the next elevator. Rushing the crowd of people, I hurried to the staircase and made my way down as fast as my shoes would allow. When I stepped out of the stairwell, I spotted Mandy.

"Where is she going?" Charlotte asked.

I'd come this far, so I decided there was no sense in turning back now. We left the track area and headed toward the barn. The horse was already at the paddocks, so I wasn't sure why Mandy was going back to the barn.

"Where is she going?" Charlotte asked again.

"Maybe she forgot something for the horse," Maureen said.

I kept my distance. If she had looked back, she would have seen me following her. I would have to think quickly to explain why. Finally, we made it to the barn. I peeked around the side of a stall. Mandy was headed toward the office.

I had to hide so that Mandy wouldn't see me. Most of the stalls were empty, so I lifted the latch on the nearest one and stepped inside.

"Cookie, be careful in there and don't step on any . . . well, horse droppings." Charlotte pointed.

I looked down at my feet. Luckily, the stall was clean. I closed the door behind me so that Mandy wouldn't notice. It was hard to stand perfectly still; I was so nervous that I was shaking. Mandy had always given me the creeps. And this time was worse. I peeked out through the space between the door and the wall.

Luckily, I had a clear view of the office from this vantage point.

"What is she looking for?" Maureen asked.

"I bet I know what she's looking for. The drugs. She probably wants to make sure they're still there." Charlotte craned her neck for a better view.

"Because she left them there on purpose," I whispered.

"Exactly," Charlotte said.

I watched as Mandy rummaged through the office.

"It looks as if she is looking for something else," Charlotte said.

"Charlotte, you should go in there and see exactly what she's up to," I said.

"Well, even though she gives me the creeps too, I guess I can do that." Charlotte left the stall.

Maureen and Ramon stayed behind with me. Just as Charlotte made it to the office door, Mandy came out. I moved back so that she wouldn't see me. I held my breath as she walked by.

"Thank goodness, she didn't look over this way," Maureen said.

Charlotte popped up beside me. "Sorry, but she took off before I got there. Now you need to go in there and see what she was looking for."

"What if she comes back?" I whispered.

"I'll see where she's going," Charlotte said.

"She's probably going back to the paddocks. They'll have to saddle the horse soon," Ramon said.

Charlotte appeared again. "She's headed back toward the track."

I released a deep breath. "I guess that means she won't come back. At least I hope she doesn't come back."

When I peeked out, I spotted Mandy. "She's still there."

"What is she doing?" Maureen whispered as if she would be heard too.

Mandy's phone rang, and she pulled it out of her pocket.

"Looks like she got a new phone," Charlotte said.

"Yes," Mandy said hastily.

"Is she ever in a good mood?" Charlotte asked.

"Now that I think about it, not really," Ramon said.

"I don't understand what he saw in her," Maureen said.

Charlotte quirked an eyebrow. "Did you look at her? She's mildly attractive. That's what he saw in her."

Maureen and Charlotte laughed, as if they were at a stand-up comedy show.

"What do you want, April?" Mandy asked. "I thought you said you were going to fix her for me."

The ghosts and I exchanged looks. I knew the woman she was speaking with had to be her best friend. She wanted her to fix me, and I knew what that meant, considering that April had been following me around.

"What do you mean you don't want to be involved? No, I didn't lie," Mandy said.

"Oh, it looks like there is trouble in best friend paradise," Charlotte said.

"Yes, trouble indeed," I whispered.

Mandy went back into the office.

"What is she doing this time?" I asked.

"I'll go look." Charlotte took off.

Only a few seconds had passed when Charlotte reappeared. "I don't know what she was doing, but she just walked by again."

I hoped she was gone for good this time. Easing the stall door open, I inched my way toward the office. When I reached the office door, I looked over my shoulder.

"She's not back there. Don't worry," Charlotte said.

I had been calm through a lot of this, but now my nerves were on edge. She'd left the office door open, so I stepped inside. Everything looked just as it had the last time I'd been in there. I scanned the room.

"You should see if the drug is still in the drawer," Maureen said.

"Good idea." When I peered down at the desk, I spotted the phone. I reached down and picked it up.

"Whose phone?" Charlotte asked.

When I swiped the screen, it lit up.

"You're not going to believe this, but Mandy left her phone again. She must have gotten a new one."

"She really can't keep up with that thing," Charlotte said.

"Is there anything new?" Maureen asked.

"You should check the text messages first," Charlotte said.

My hand shook as I touched the screen to get the messages to pop up. "There are no text messages that stand out as unusual."

"Check the email and the photos," Charlotte instructed.

I moved to the photos first. I had already looked last time, of course, but maybe there was something new.

"She should really look into password-protecting that phone," Maureen said.

"I'm glad she hasn't done that," I said.

"She's not as smart as she thinks she is," Charlotte said.

"Uh-oh," I said as I looked at the screen.

"What's that?" Charlotte asked, stepping closer.

"How did I not notice this in the photos last time?"

"What is it?" Maureen asked with excitement.

"There are photos I didn't see last time."

Maureen pretended to cover her eyes. "I'm almost afraid to find out what they are," she said.

"Mandy is a hot mess," Charlotte said. "That being said, let's see the photos."

"There's a photo of Mandy at the event where Ramon was murdered."

"And?" Ramon asked as he moved closer.

"Well, it's what Mandy is wearing that caught my attention."

"Please tell me she is wearing clothing," Maureen said.

"Oh, I couldn't handle having that sight burned into my retinas." Charlotte shivered.

"She's wearing the bracelet."

"The one that Danielle had?" Ramon asked.

I nodded. "That's the one."

"Danielle did say that Mandy had stolen stuff from her. Maybe she stole that bracelet," Charlotte said.

"Wouldn't Danielle have noticed Mandy wearing it that day?" I asked.

"Yes, I think I would have noticed," Charlotte said.

"There was a lot going on. Maybe she didn't pay attention," Maureen said. "Or maybe she only wore it when Danielle wasn't around."

I looked through more photos on the phone. I stopped on the next one. "Whoa."

"What is it?" Charlotte and Maureen asked in unison.

"There's a photo of Mandy at the event."

"Well, we knew she was there," Charlotte said.

"Yes, but she took a photo of the area where Ramon was murdered."

"Maybe she was morbidly fascinated after I died," Ramon said.

"That's not the case," I said. "She snapped a photo of Ramon's back as he went into the restroom."

"So she was waiting for him when he came out?" Charlotte asked.

My stomach dropped. "Yes, it seems that is the case."

"So she was there and had the bracelet too. She lost the bracelet when she killed Ramon. I think she was there to watch him die and wanted to take a photo to remember the event," Charlotte said.

"That is disturbing," I said.

"I guess I think differently about Mandy now," Ramon said.

"Yes, I guess you do," Charlotte said.

"I had no idea she would do something like this to me."

"We understand how you feel," Maureen said. "We've all been murdered. We'll never understand the sick minds of our murderers."

"What do we do now?" Ramon asked.

I placed the phone in my purse. "I have to get this to Dylan. After that, we can go to the police with it. I'm sure Dylan is getting worried about me now."

"I hope she doesn't come back for the phone before you can get out of here," Charlotte said.

That was why I needed to get out of there right away.

"There's no time to look to see if the drug is still in the drawer."

"I guess Mandy put it there so that the police would think Elise had killed Ramon," Maureen said.

"I suppose she was growing impatient, waiting for the police to find it," I said.

I hurried over to the door and stepped outside. I left the door open just as Mandy had.

"Do you have the phone?" Charlotte asked.

"Yes, I have it in my pocket."

The thunderous sound of hooves rushed by.

"I think they sense your stress," Charlotte said.

"Wait. I see someone coming," Ramon said.

I immediately stopped, pressing my body up against the barn.

"Who is it?" I whispered.

"Oh, it's just a man going to a different barn," Ramon said.

Whew. I released my pent-up breath. "Is it safe to go now?"

"Yes, it's all clear," Ramon said.

I rounded the side of the barn. Now I had to get across the lot without running into Mandy. Maybe she wouldn't realize she had lost her phone. Yes, I forgot that she was probably busy with the horse. That meant I wouldn't have to worry about running into her right now. I made it over to the tree that grew by the entrance that led back to the track. The next thing I knew I had been hit on the back of the head. I tumbled to the ground.

Chapter 32

Cookie's Savvy Tips for Vintage Shopping

There's a ton of wonderful vintage costume jewelry out there just waiting for you to discover it.

"Cookie, are you okay?" Charlotte yelled. "Look out. Here she comes again."

Mandy wrapped something around my neck. She pulled me back with it, and I was choking. I reached for my neck to try and loosen whatever was constricting my neck and throat.

"She's choking you with the horse reins," Ramon yelled.

I was gasping for air. I had to think of something before it was too late. I probably had only seconds before I would black out. Clawing at the leather strap was doing nothing. I couldn't get my fingers between the reins and my skin so that I could get air. I had no idea she was so strong. I had to think of something else.

Obviously, I couldn't stop her this way. The more I struggled, the worse it got.

"We have to do something," Charlotte said.

I'd never heard her so panicked. The ghosts were moving around, trying to help. They grabbed at Mandy, but it was having no effect.

"I've never seen a more evil face," Maureen said.

I couldn't believe this was the way I was going to die. I'd put myself in danger, and now I couldn't get out. What could I do to stop her? I tried to kick up, but that did nothing either. I punched her from over my head, but it did nothing.

I remembered I was wearing a hat pin. If only I could reach it. I would have to move swiftly though because she might try to stop me. Either way, she would have to loosen her grip. In one swift movement, I reached up for my hat. I couldn't believe it, but I made contact with the pin right away and pulled it from the hat. With all my strength, I jabbed the hat pin toward Mandy. She screamed out, and the leather reins dropped from my throat.

"Oh, Cookie, I can't believe it. Run," Charlotte said.

I scrambled up from the ground. The hat pin had landed in Mandy's cheek.

"She's really mad now," Ramon said.

Yeah, well, I was a little agitated too. I ran from

the barn. I had to get the police. Or just anyone. Someone to help me stop this madwoman. With one quick yank, Mandy had pulled the hat pin from her face. She was coming after me.

"Run faster, Cookie," Maureen said.

I'd love to have run faster, but my legs didn't have a big stride. Mandy had longer legs, and she moved like a gazelle.

"Here she comes, Cookie," Charlotte yelled.

Movement from my right caught my attention. Like a streak of lightning, Dylan appeared. He ran past us and tackled Mandy. They fell to the ground with a thud.

"Wow, that was impressive," Maureen said.

Dylan had managed to subdue Mandy, although she was still struggling to get up.

"Cookie, can you get me those reins?" Dylan motioned with a tilt of his head.

He was still holding Mandy's hands behind her back. I ran over and grabbed the weapon she'd just used to try to murder me. How ironic that now she was being tied up with it. Dylan got Mandy up to a sitting position.

"I'd like my phone back now." Her voice was full of venom and hate.

I handed it to Dylan. "I think the police would like to look at it first."

Ramon was standing beside me. "I guess now I can tell you."

I whispered out of the corner of my mouth, "Tell me what?"

"Mandy believed in witchcraft. We went to the occult store together. That stuff spooked me though. I didn't want to know what she was doing."

"Now you're telling me this?"

"Mandy, you sent me the strange poem and the note?" I asked.

"It wasn't me." She glared.

"Who was it?"

I didn't believe anything she said.

An evil smile spread across her face. "It was April. She does anything I tell her to do."

I looked at Dylan. "Mandy placed the drugs in Elise's office, hoping that Elise would be arrested for the murder. She stole a lot of things from Danielle, and probably a lot of other people too. She lost the bracelet at the crime scene. She even took a photo of Ramon right before she murdered him."

"You have no proof of that," Mandy said.

"There is proof on your phone," I said.

"I didn't leave the drugs in the desk drawer." Mandy struggled to get free.

"How did you know that was where it was?" I asked.

She glared at me. "You should mind your own business."

"Why did you do it?" Dylan asked.

She smirked. "Ramon deserved what he got."

"What?" Ramon yelled. "I did nothing to deserve that."

Dylan saw me looking over at the tree. He probably wondered if I'd lost my mind.

"You tried to kill me too," I said.

"You were snooping around too much."

At least she had admitted it. Thank goodness, the police arrived to take Mandy away. Her glare was creeping me out. The officer led her toward the police car. Mandy stared at me for as long as possible. She gave up when they stuffed her into the backseat of the car. Mandy would probably watch me from there too.

"Did she hurt you?" Dylan stroked my cheek with the palm of his hand.

I rubbed my neck. "Well, my neck is kind of sore, but I should be okay. I'm glad you came along when you did. I would have had to fight her again."

"Looks like you did a pretty good job of it."

"Well, thanks to my vintage hat pin."

The police still needed to talk with us.

The young detective approached. "Can you tell me what happened?"

"I can tell you." Charlotte held up her hand.

Maureen waved her hand in front of Charlotte's face. "Remember, he can't hear you."

Charlotte slumped her shoulders. "Oh yeah."

"Well, here goes. The whole story. I was hiding so that Mandy wouldn't see me. Mandy left her phone on the desk in the office."

"For someone who loves social media so much,

she sure can't keep up with her phone," Charlotte said.

I continued, "I looked through the phone and noticed something odd. There were photos, and in one I spotted the bracelet on Mandy's wrist. The one found at the murder scene. The photo was taken the day of Ramon's murder. But there was another photo taken at the location of the scene of the crime. Ramon was in the background, so he was alive at that time. That placed Mandy at the scene of the crime just before he was killed."

The officer stared at me. When I looked at Dylan, he smiled.

The officer nodded. "Okay, we'll be in touch if we have more questions."

"Oh, they'll have more questions all right. Cookie solved the crime," Charlotte said with pride in her voice.

After speaking with the officer, Dylan and I got a chance to see the race from right there by the rail. The track was a good distance away, but we still felt the excitement as the horses and jockeys went by.

"The horse won," I yelled, jumping up and down.

The ghosts were jumping up and down too.

"Despite Mandy trying to interfere with the training," Dylan said.

"They should have fired her a long time ago," I said.

The officers were nice enough to let us watch the race before asking us questions again. I couldn't believe the horse had won. Now if I could just get a chance to go back over and talk with everyone. They probably didn't miss us though, with all the excitement of the win.

As we stood there watching the police escort Mandy away, it sounded as if someone whispered, trying to get my attention. I peered over my shoulder. Corbin, the horse groomer who had disappeared, was standing by the barn. He motioned for me to come over. I hurried over without saying a word to Dylan, who was still busy talking with the police.

"Is he hiding from the police?" Charlotte asked.

"I guess we're about to find out," I said.

"Corbin, what are you doing here?" I asked.

"Is it safe to come out now?" he whispered.

"Safe from what?"

"From Mandy."

My eyes widened. "Do you mean that you've been hiding because of her?"

"That's terrible," Charlotte said.

"I was afraid she wanted to kill me," Corbin said.

"Why would she want to kill you?" I asked.

"Just because she's plain mean."

I certainly couldn't deny that.

"You're safe now," I said. "She left in the police car."

Corbin stepped out from the side of the building.

"How long have you been hiding here?"

"Oh no, I wasn't hiding here," he said. "I went out of town."

"So what made you come back?" I asked.

"Well, I just missed it here, and I was going to go to the police. I wanted to see if there wasn't something I could do to stop her."

"Did you know that she killed Ramon?"

Corbin shook his head. "I wasn't sure, but I had my suspicions. I should have said something to the police," he said.

"Actually, some people thought that maybe you had killed Ramon."

"Yeah, like you," Charlotte said.

His eyes widened. "I did it? Why would I kill Ramon? I liked him."

"I liked you too, buddy," Ramon said.

"What happened to you?" Corbin asked.

I knew I looked as if I'd been in a hurricane.

Charlotte stepped forward. "Well, as Cookie was leaving, someone attacked her from behind. Mandy was trying to choke her with a horse's reins. It looked as if the poem Cookie found was about to come true." Charlotte waved her hands. "There was a struggle, but Cookie managed to use the hat pin from her vintage hat to stab Mandy. That allowed her to get away. Thank heavens, Dylan had been looking for Cookie. Luckily, he arrived just in time to subdue Mandy until the local police arrived."

Charlotte had forgotten that Corbin couldn't hear a word of what she'd just said.

"I stabbed Mandy in the face with a hat pin."

Corbin's mouth dropped open. "Well, at least you got away from her."

"Yes, and you're safe now," I said.

"So they really arrested Mandy?" Corbin asked.

"She's been handcuffed, and soon she'll be on her way to jail," I said.

"Now that makes me happy," Charlotte said.

"Everything seems so final now," Corbin said, looking down at his shoes.

I supposed the reality had set in now.

"Thanks for everything, Ms. Chanel. I'm going to find everyone and let them know I'm back."

"They'll be happy to see you." I smiled.

Corbin took off for the track. Dylan was watching me, so I walked back over.

"Everything okay?" Dylan asked.

"Just fine," I said.

We talked with the police for a bit longer. When they drove Mandy away, it was as if the dark cloud over us dissipated. Danielle sent a text to find out where I was. She wanted me to join them at the winner's circle. I never thought I'd be at the winner's circle at Churchill Downs. She had no idea that Mandy had attacked me and that she had been arrested.

Dylan and I made our way to the winner's circle. It was much larger than it appeared on TV. The smell of flowers and dirt filled the air. Brightly colored tulips decorated the area. The excitement was thick. People gathered around the horse and jockey. Cameras and reporters asked questions before we posed for a photo with the winning horse.

"It's all over," I said.

"What's over?" Danielle asked.

"Mandy has been arrested for Ramon's murder."

"You're kidding? What happened? You look as if you've been in a fight." Danielle looked me up and down.

With the dirt on my dress and my hair rumpled, I knew I looked terrible.

"Actually, I was in a fight. Danielle, I overheard Lewis tell Elise that he didn't want anyone to know what they were doing. What did he mean by that?"

She laughed. "He was just talking about the horse training. They're doing special training that they don't want the competition to know about. Heart rate monitors and stuff."

"See, I told you, Cookie," Charlotte said.

Charlotte had been just as suspicious as me. That was neither here nor there now though.

I explained to everyone what had happened. The hat pin to the cheek and all. I knew the police would be waiting to talk with everyone. Even with all the excitement, I was glad that I was finally going home.

"It's Big Red." Ramon pointed.

"Secretariat?" Charlotte asked.

I followed his pointing finger. A misty tunnel appeared beside one of the barns. It was as if the horse was waiting for someone.

"I think it's time for me to go," Ramon said as he moved toward the tunnel.

"Secretariat came for Ramon," Charlotte whispered.

"That's beautiful," Maureen said.

"Bye, Ramon." I waved.

"Thank you, Cookie. Without you I would have never been able to leave."

Ramon walked to the tunnel. A second later, he disappeared right into it. It was as if the thing had never been there. Now it was just Charlotte and Maureen. Charlotte moved between the worlds. She had a special talent for it. She wasn't going anywhere for long. She might go away for a while, but she always came back.

As I stood there, absorbing all of the excitement and chaos from the event, my cell phone rang. My mother's number popped up on the screen. She had impeccable timing. If I didn't answer, she would just keep calling, so I picked up.

I yelled into the phone. "I can't hear you right now. It's really loud here. I think that I might be on TV."

"I see you," my mother screamed into the phone.

"I'll have to call you back." I waved so that she could see me.

"Wait, don't hang up. They found Maureen's killer."

"What's that?" I yelled.

"I said, they found Maureen's killer."

"Who was it?" This time I yelled because I was shocked at the news.

"The woman who had an affair with her husband," my mother said.

"Did the police arrest her?"

"Yes, they did. I'll explain later."

"Wow, I guess that was a lot of excitement for everyone. I'll call you soon when I can hear better," I said.

Now I had to explain to Maureen exactly what had happened. It was just as Grandma Pearl had said. Charlotte and Maureen were staring at me.

"Well?" Charlotte said. "We overheard you talking. Give us the details."

I couldn't talk to them right there in front of everybody, and especially not on national television. I wouldn't want to embarrass anyone like that. I'd have to explain to Danielle why the crazy woman with her was talking to herself.

I touched Dylan's arm. "I'll be right back. I just need to step over here and call my mother back. I couldn't hear her."

"Well, if you think it's important, sure, you should call her back," Dylan said.

He probably figured my mother wanted to give me a new tofu cookie recipe or something. Normally, I would've thought the same thing.

Somehow, I made my way to the edge of the track. I would pretend to talk on my cell phone so that no one would be suspicious.

"Okay, now tell us what's going on," Charlotte said.

"I'm almost too nervous to find out." Maureen shifted from one foot to the other.

I stared at the women. "They found the killer and arrested her for Maureen's death. Yes, it was the woman who was having an affair with your husband."

"That low-down, rotten, disgusting human being." Maureen shook her fist.

"Let it all out," Charlotte said. "Let that anger out."

"So what are you going to do now?" Charlotte asked Maureen.

She was quiet, as if she was contemplating her next step.

"There's only one thing for me to do now," she said.

"What's that?" I asked.

"It's time for me to leave."

"What! I go in and out of this world, and so can you," Charlotte said.

"That's for you, Charlotte. I could never do that. I always said when they found the killer, I would leave immediately, and that's exactly what I'm going to do."

Over by the entrance to the track, I spotted the light misty tunnel. It was just like the one that had appeared for Ramon. There was no horse this time, although there were a few people.

"There's my family," Maureen said.

I nodded. "I understand, Maureen. I'll miss you."

She waved and walked toward the tunnel without looking back. She was brave. Charlotte and I stood there watching the area where Maureen had disappeared.

"Well, I guess that's that," Charlotte said.

"I'm going to miss her," I said. "Aren't you, Charlotte?"

She shrugged. I could read her expression. Charlotte would miss Maureen too.

"I'm sure I'll run into her on the other side occasionally," Charlotte said.

"Do you have cell phones there? Never mind." I waved my hand.

Sadness set in every time one of the ghosts had to leave. As much as I complained when they first showed up, they were like friends by the time they left. That was life, and I had to deal with it.

After returning to the crowded area, I found Dylan again. As we stood in the winner's circle, I wondered about Ken. I hadn't seen him since I'd left the room to follow Mandy. Had he taken off? I asked Danielle, but she said she hadn't seen him for a bit. I wanted to say good-bye before he left to go back to Sugar Creek. I hoped he wasn't mad at me. After we were finished at the winner's circle, everyone was going back to the barn to say goodbye to the horse. Dylan and I walked from the track to the barn together.

As we neared the barn, I noticed a few people across the way. That was when I realized one of them was Ken. He was getting into a truck with two men. What was going on?

I touched Dylan's arm. "Something doesn't seem right. Ken is getting in a truck with the two men who were following me. I think we should go over and ask what's wrong."

Dylan stared at me. "Okay, let's go find out."

We approached the truck as the driver was getting in. Ken was sitting in the middle, looking like a hostage.

"Hey, you." I yelled. "What are you doing?"

Ken noticed me. He looked as if he was pleading for help. The guy jumped in and cranked the engine, but it wouldn't start.

"Get out of the truck," Dylan yelled.

The men had nowhere to go. When Dylan flashed his badge, the men stepped out from the truck.

"Put your hands up," Dylan commanded.

"What's the matter, officer?" the driver asked.

Ken got out of the truck too. He placed his hands up as if he'd done something wrong. "These were the guys who were following Cookie. They were trying to intimidate me. I don't know where they were going to take me."

"Do you work for Mandy?" I asked the men.

They didn't answer. Instead they exchanged a look with each other. I took that as a yes.

"Turn around and place your hands on the truck. No sudden movements." Dylan moved over to the men. "You're under arrest."

Dylan called for police backup. There certainly had been a lot of arrests here today.

"Thank you, Cookie and Dylan, for saving me. I don't know where these guys were taking me."

"Glad I could help, but it wasn't me. Cookie is the one you should thank. I wouldn't have even noticed you getting in the truck," Dylan said.

What Dylan probably meant to say was that he wouldn't have done anything even if he had noticed Ken. Not that Dylan wouldn't have wanted to save Ken; it was just that he wouldn't have realized that Ken was in trouble. The cops arrived and arrested the men. Dylan said they would be charged with kidnapping. Plus, there would be charges for stalking me.

Dylan pulled me to the side. "Cookie, there's something I want to talk to you about."

"What's that?" I asked. "You're starting to worry me."

Charlotte stood close so that she could hear more clearly. Plus we were anxious to hear what he had to say.

"There's something I've been wanting to talk to you about, but I just didn't know how to bring it up." Dylan ran his hand through his hair.

He always did that when he was nervous, which wasn't often.

"He's going to ask her to marry him," Charlotte practically squealed.

"The other day, I know I heard you talking to someone in your hotel room."

"Oh no, he thinks you're cheating on him. This is terrible." Charlotte twisted her hands. "I can't watch."

"And that's not all," Dylan said. "Apparently, you left me a voice mail without even realizing it. I heard a conversation. Who were you talking to when you were in the office barn?"

"Oh no. He must have heard you talking to us. There's only one thing you can do, Cookie," Charlotte said. "You have to tell him the truth."

My anxiety rose, and my heart sped up.

"You mentioned the word 'ghosts.' What did you mean by that?" Dylan studied my face.

Charlotte was right yet again. I had to tell Dylan the truth. The time had finally come. I couldn't lie to him any longer. If that meant he never wanted to talk to me again, then so be it. What was the point if he didn't like me for me?

Charlotte stared.

"Well, here goes," I said.

Dylan quirked an eyebrow.

"Oh, I almost can't listen. Almost," Charlotte said.

"Dylan, something strange happened a while back. I saw a ghost."

He didn't laugh, and he didn't smile. His expression didn't change.

"I don't think he believes you," Charlotte said. "He probably thinks you're joking."

"It happened with the ghost of Charlotte Meadows. It's been happening with other spirits too."

"That's why you were asking about Maureen's death," he said.

I nodded. "I know it sounds crazy, but it's the truth."

"Wait until you tell him that the cat is actually your grandmother," Charlotte said with a chuckle.

Dylan took my hands into his. "I believe you."

My mouth dropped. "You do?"

He nodded. "Yes, I believe in the paranormal."

"As sure as corn bread goes with greens, he's the man of your dreams," Charlotte said.

An Excerpt from Cookie's Blog

Vintage Clothing You Need Now!

When shopping for vintage, here's a quick look at items that should be on your "must have" list.

- Cigarette pants
- Pedal pushers
- A-line skirts
- Pencil skirts
- Cardigan sweaters
- Hats
- Slips

All of these items are considered timeless and classic. They can be incorporated into your modern wardrobe. The items can be casual or worn for work, even formal events. Imagine how versatile your wardrobe can be by adding just a few vintage items.

For example, pedal pushers can be worn with heels or flats . . . even sneakers, for a super casual look. The same can be said about the cigarette pants. Pencil skirts can be worn to the office or for date night. With the right blouse, a pencil skirt could even take you to that glamorous cocktail party.

Acknowledgments

Many thanks to my husband for his insight into the world of thoroughbred racing. Also thank you to my editor, Michaela Hamilton, and my agent, Jill Marsal.

Don't miss Rose Pressey's next delightful
Haunted Vintage Mystery

A Passion for Haunted Fashion

Coming soon from Kensington Publishing Corp.
Keep reading to enjoy a sample excerpt . . .

Chapter 1

There were rumors that the Sugar Creek Theater was haunted. Most of the lights had stopped working in the basement of the building years ago. Fixing them wasn't a top priority for management. Against my better judgment, I headed toward the costume room. It was located down in the dungeon. At least that was what I called the space. The floorboards creaked with every step I took. Every time I came down here, I felt as if someone was watching my every move. That was why I hadn't come alone today.

I'd never given much thought to ghosts until they started talking to me.

I'd brought a ghost with me today. Charlotte Meadows wouldn't miss out on tagging along. She was bossy and loved telling me what to do. Charlotte had been with me for a while now, ever since I'd found her at an estate sale. She'd been attached to her clothing. We'd been through a lot together in a short amount of time. Now she refused to move on from this dimension.

"Cookie, don't forget to put Heather in bright colors. She's always so blah." Her gold bangles clanged together as Charlotte talked with her hands.

"I'm glad Heather can't hear you say that."

Charlotte eased down the hallway beside me. She watched every step she took in her black four-inch Christian Louboutin heels, as if she thought she might take a wrong step on the old floor.

"Charlotte, it's okay if you fall . . . you're already dead. What can it hurt?"

"Why do you insist on reminding me of that every day?" Charlotte asked.

"It's just a fact," I said.

"Besides, it could hurt my ego," she said.

As usual, Charlotte's chestnut-colored hair fell to her shoulders in perfect waves, as if she'd just stepped out of a salon. Her makeup was photograph-ready, and her white Chanel blouse and black Louis Vuitton skirt were the latest off the runway. Charlotte knew fashion, no matter if she was dead. She didn't go for vintage like me though.

We continued down the hallway. Footsteps sounded from behind me. A cold breeze drifted across my skin.

"Charlotte, stop goofing around. I've noticed your shoes. There's no reason to exaggerate your footsteps."

"That's not me," she whispered.

I froze. If the sound hadn't come from Charlotte's feet, then who was making the noise? I eased around, completely expecting to see someone else behind us. No one was there.

"This place really is haunted. I don't like ghosts." Charlotte rubbed her arms, as if fighting off goose bumps.

That was hilarious considering Charlotte was a specter. I refrained from reminding her of that once again.

At the end of the hallway was the room reserved for all the costumes. Racks and racks of vintage clothing, handmade costumes, and various props filled the space. As soon as I entered the area, the sense that someone was watching fell over me again.

"Why did they stick you down here in this creepy space? There are no windows. One of these nights they will forget you're down here and lock you in."

"Thanks, Charlotte, as if I wasn't scared enough already."

The spookiness was forgotten when I started sorting through the clothing. Vintage always made me feel better and eased my troubles. Clothing from bygone days was my thing. I owned a boutique in Sugar Creek, Georgia, called It's Vintage Y'all. When I got my hands on a 1950s hoop skirt or a 1940s party dress, all my stress oozed away. A gorgeous Dior cocktail dress made all my troubles vanish. Anything Chanel made my heart go pitty-pat. Considering my name is Cookie Chanel,

I suppose that was fitting. When, as a child, I ate an entire package of cookies, my Grandma Pearl gave me the nickname Cookie. The moniker fit so well with Chanel that it stuck.

Charlotte sat on an old trunk in the corner of the room. "What do you need for the costume? Let's get this going so we can get out of here."

"You know, Charlotte, you didn't have to come down here." I pulled out a bright fuchsia and black floral-print dress and examined it.

It had spaghetti straps, a full skirt, and a fitted waist, and the cut and fabric would be fabulous on my best friend, Heather Sweet. The director had put me in charge of costumes for Sugar Creek Theater's production of *Cat on a Hot Tin Roof*. Heather had the role of Maggie.

"I can't leave you alone down here. What if a ghost gets you?" Charlotte studied her red-polished fingernails.

She didn't seem all that concerned.

"I suppose I'll talk to the ghost, just like I do with you," I said.

Charlotte pinned me with a frosty stare. "You just had to get in the fact that I'm dead, didn't you?"

I moved away from the rack and closer to Charlotte. "I'm just sayin' . . ."

She jumped up from the trunk. "Pick out a dress, and let's get a move on. How about that one?"

"Which one?" I asked.

Charlotte gestured with a flick of her wrist. "The one that looks like the dress you're wearing."

I pulled the frock from the rack. The fabric was

similar to the dress I'd worn today. The butterflies on the fabric were smaller than the ones on mine. The colors were the same hues of lilac and yellow. The V-neck bodice had a nipped waist, and the tea-length skirt was full.

I placed it back on the stand. "Heather already has a dress with these colors."

Charlotte massaged her temples, as if ghosts could really have headaches. "Just pick something already."

"What's in that trunk?" I pointed.

"How should I know," Charlotte said.

I reached down and examined the latch. "It's not locked."

"That's not an invitation to open it. There's probably a mouse in there."

Just in case Charlotte was right about the vermin, I eased the lid open. So far, no rodents. However, I'd found some seriously fabulous vintage clothing. Who left these wonderful pieces? A 1950s fitted black cocktail dress with a low back. A 1940s sleeveless sweater in a gorgeous cream color. Everything was from the 1950s, with exception of a few pieces from the 1940s.

"Is that cashmere?" Charlotte leaned closer.

Now Charlotte was interested.

"Did you see this trunk yesterday?" I asked.

Charlotte tapped her foot against the dinged-up floor. "With all this junk, how would I remember? Now let's go."

"I think that dress is beautiful." The female voice carried across the room.

I jumped, tossing the dress in the air. When I spun around, I saw a young woman standing by the door. She was probably about five years younger than me, around twenty-five. She had brown hair cut into a bob, with bouncy curls that framed her round face. Her mint-colored dress looked like it had been made in the 1950s. A large bow adorned the neckline, and the fitted waist flowed into a gathered full skirt. I was almost sure the dress had been handmade by a talented seam-stress. Maybe my style was having an influence on people around town. Where had she come from? It was as if she'd appeared out of nowhere.

"The trunk belongs to me," she said. "I've been stuck in this building for years."

Oh no. Another ghost?

Connect with Us

Visit us online at
KensingtonBooks.com
to read more from your favorite authors, see books
by series, view reading group guides, and more.

for sneak peeks, chances to win books and prize packs,
and to share your thoughts with other readers.

facebook.com/kensingtonpublishing
twitter.com/kensingtonbooks

Tell us what you think!

To share your thoughts, submit a review,
or sign up for our eNewsletters, please visit:
KensingtonBooks.com/TellUs.